Yxu

Morning in Antibes

By John Knowles

A Separate Peace
Morning in Antibes

Morning in Antibes

A Novel by

JOHN KNOWLES

New York   *THE MACMILLAN COMPANY*   *1962*

First Printing

The Macmillan Company, New York
Brett-Macmillan Ltd., Galt, Ontario

Printed in the United States of America

Library of Congress catalog card number: 62–7519

Morning in Antibes

||||||||||||||||||||||||||||||||||||||||||||||||||||||||||||||||||||||||| The
next morning—moist, shining, and still—I awoke in the shadowy
bedroom. The hard sunshine outside was reflected around the room
and gave an underwater density to the atmosphere. I was alone; the
others had left late at night and taken all their urges with them,
and mine too, for the time being. I lay still in the bright and shadowy room, and these urges were for a few minutes like the blue
canvas shorts on the chair, the clean white T-shirt beside them, the
canvas espadrilles on the floor, waiting patiently to be put on for
the day.

The bedroom was still. I lay back on the long and firm roll the
French use instead of a pillow, and felt the steady harmonious pull
of morning on the Mediterranean. The dawn never broke here; instead it commenced with a regular rolling energy, like a tide coming
slowly and deliberately in.

Outside the large window was a rose tree, as unreal and bewitched as Jack's beanstalk. It stood alone in a pool of raked gravel, with a serviceable trunk supporting an umbrella fullness of branches and leaves—and roses, dozens of huge and blood-bright roses, growing on a tree.

Beyond the tree, villas and apartment houses with orange tile roofs dwindled off among groves of slim umbrella pines; the pines were fixed in thin greenness against the overwhelming morning blue of the sky. The sun seemed to be motionless too on this motionless morning; it poured steadily and caressingly down, different from other sunshine because here nothing whatever obstructed it, not so much as one trailing wisp of cloud anywhere in the sky, nothing, emptiness, an endless shimmer of blue motionless sky.

Along the street under my window, which was lined with these rose trees, was a commencing morning breaker of life. The metal screen that shielded the window of the grocery store opposite clattered up; the grocer came rattling through the curtain of beads hanging in his door, scrapingly put down two big milk cans on the sidewalk, called, "Okay, old man?" to the doorkeeper of my apartment house in a garlic voice, and then went rattling back through the beads.

The first motor scooter of the day tore aggressively by, backfired at the corner, and surged off toward the beach. Silence again, an undertow drew the noise back away for a little while, and then a fresh wave broke, a small one, the little sewing-machine whir of a car called the Two-Horse, sputtering experimentally down to the corner.

I turned over and poured a glass of a mineral water called Badoit from a bottle beside the bed. It had the taste of health.

A horse clomped by, tired already, pulling a wagon that wheezed and squeaked, a large one, too large for the horse. This wagon went by every morning. . . .

It had been going by when I first arrived at the Gilded Pine apartment house, a month before, running away—as other people ran away from bad weather—from bad love.

The wagon had squeaked past, and I had stepped out of the taxi

2

from the airport, still a little spellbound from the first immersion in the Mediterranean air, still looking sharply around now and then to be sure something miraculous wasn't happening behind me, the mountains growing, for instance, or the road being rolled up like a rug by people on motor scooters. The taxi had picked me up at the airport and hurtled along a fast road bordering the sea, traffic moving fast and noisily both ways, Rolls-Royces and bicycles, rumbling trucks and little Two-Horses; on the right a temporary crop of campers' tents, on the left a flashing inlet of the sea; on the right a town, old as crime, hanging to a theatrical mount and spilling down its side to expire in a row of cheap cafés along the road as we sped past, on the left overturned fishermen's boats and their nets and their men, all resting in the sun; on the right a big bright gas station; on the left and some distance away, lower than the road, a fort on the edge of the water; on the right another fort, its walls hanging over the road; then through a tunnel of trees, over a railroad pass, into a side street, through a little square, along a mercantile avenue into a very important square with calculated flower beds in the center and first-class cafés around the edge, along a broad street, up an incline, down the other side with large, spaced trees always on both sides, into a cool, moist little resort, a right turn into a street lined incredibly with trees blooming roses, and then we stopped before a large dreaming building in pale yellow, with its name, the Gilded Pine, inset over the door and a red tile terrace, as a tired horse clomped by pulling a squeaking wagon that was too big for it.

The wagon passed.

In a stone arcade on the second story of a large house next door a little girl I had never seen but heard every morning began to sing again, "La-la-la, lalalala, la-la-la . . ." I thought of her not too affectionately as a little ray of morning sunshine. Her voice was so sweet and so innocent that she sounded like an impersonation of a little girl singing. While she sang I put the apartment into motion again—switched on the hot-water heater, turned the gas for the stove on, and threw the lever so that there would be electricity. I

3

put on some swimming trunks while the coffee was heating, went across to get a piece of ice for the icebox from the grocer, bought *Nice Matin* at the tobacco shop next door, glanced at the headline: THE COMMITTEE OF PUBLIC SAFETY IN ALGERIA PROCLAIMS IT WILL ACCEPT ONLY A GOVERNMENT HEADED BY GENERAL DE GAULLE, came back and drank the coffee mixed with hot milk and ate a piece of hard bread and marmalade, and then walked down through the town and dived into the Mediterranean Sea. The water was cold enough to wake me completely and warm enough so that I could have stayed in an hour. The sun was at the point where no one thought about it, just as no one thinks about flawless health. Beach boys were raking the white sand. I got out and began to dry myself. The sea was distilled blue when I looked at it with my head leaning to the right, quicksilver with sun reflections when I leaned to the left. The air smelled of sea and pine needles. It insisted on good health. At the end of the day it would smell of sea and pine needles, mingled with the smell of garlic and Gauloise cigarettes; then it would blare desire.

I felt the stickiness of Mediterranean salt on my skin, and I felt the impulsions of Juan-les-Pins waiting patiently for me at the next corner; when I turned it they would fall into step like a genial old friend. By the end of the day, when the garlic and Gauloises had drifted into the air, this old friend would have me by the throat.

I sat down as usual at the Café Victory for breakfast. The sun blazed on the sea so blindingly that I had to change chairs and put my back to it. I leafed through the rest of the newspaper, pausing only to scan a story headed:

A NORTH AFRICAN, 27, IS STABBED ON THE BEACH OF ANTIBES THEN THROWN INTO THE SEA

HIS CADAVER HAS BEEN BROUGHT BACK TO SHORE BY SOME FISHERMEN

WAS HE THE VICTIM OF A SETTLING OF POLITICAL ACCOUNTS?

4

Sergio came as usual with orange juice, coffee and milk, and a half-moon roll called a *croissant*. "The sea is good, as usual?"

I said it certainly was.

He stood in his white jacket, white towel over his arm, dark narrow pants, and one foot turned outward so that the pointed Italian toe of his shoe was aimed at my chair. His face was calmly and carefully set, and the new calculation in him was just beginning to appear at the corners of his eyes. He watched me while I tasted the coffee. "The coffee is good, very good today," I said. He relaxed, both toes turned outward contentedly, his wide smile grew a little wider, and he said, "Well, when you grind it yourself that makes all the difference." His slim flared nose sniffed the sea, and then he asked me if I wanted to change any money. I gained about twenty cents on every dollar by changing money with Sergio instead of with the French government.

"Yes. Twenty dollars."

"That's all right."

"I'll bring you the travelers' checks this afternoon."

"Right."

Our business was settled; it was time for general conversation.

"How are your projects going?" I asked.

He fingered his thin mustache, his mouth opening and eyebrows going up philosophically, and he said, "They're going, they're going." Was he going to discuss them? I waited while he asked himself that, his dark wide-set eyes wandering across the perfect sky. "My former mistress—you remember my telling you about that Parisian girl I had last summer—she has returned. Naturally my fiancée must not see her. That Parisian girl wishes to become a professional now. She got married during the winter. It didn't work. She's much too hysterical to be married, you know. She had her baby two months ago. Now she doesn't know how to meet the proper man. I am going to do that for her, I think."

"Ah, well . . ."

"I can get a lot of cash that way, and fast. She is very good, one

5

of the best I ever slept with." His eyes lost their dreaming philoso-
phizing in the sky; they sharpened and came into focus; his gaze
slid down the horizon, down the latticework and flowerpots to me.
"Yes, I suppose she is the best I ever had in bed. Frankly. My
fiancée is different, spiritual. I tell you one thing, this Parisian, she
knows how to make love! You, for example, might enjoy . . ." his
hands spread, his head cocked, and the proposition was articulated
in one sound, gently guttural: "Eh?"

"Me? Why should I pay for it. Eh?"

"Ah, yes," his voice dropped the question, "that's so. Why should
you?" He began to think about other prospects, quietly picking his
teeth, a small muscle flicking in his jaw. His hand with the tooth-
pick trembled very slightly. His engagement seemed to have
tilted Sergio a little out of equilibrium, as though there were un-
settling rollers turning slowly but constantly under his feet.

"Well, Sergio," I said, "you'll arrange everything for yourself."

"Ye-e-e-s," he said in a knowing, confident growl.

The day progressed. The blondes began to descend from their
white hotels, clip-clopping under the palm trees, their stomachs
swelling slightly above the little V of their bathing pants, and two
cups holding their breasts in place. Skin was on parade for the day,
smooth and evenly tanned skin, and it was the same even if the
blonde had a daughter of fourteen coming along with her. The
French bathing suit was invented because aging women discovered that the skin in the middle of the body often remained
soft, and that part of the body shapely, after the arms and legs
had begun to coarsen and sag. They were all contenders, wives and
mothers for twenty years or not; they were still in training for love.
Women withdrew from Juan-les-Pins when they weren't sexual
contenders any more, went to Nice or into retirement with whatever winnings they had. In the casino there were roulette and
chemin de fer and boule, but these were child's play to the real
gamblers of Juan-les-Pins, who played not for money but for love,
with their bodies as stakes. That's why Liliane was here, and why
I was here.

6

She came along, shiningly dark-haired among the blondes. We shook hands, and she said with her optimistic smile, "Did you have a nice evening?"

"We had dinner in Old Antibes."

"Yes, so I heard."

So there was no chance to lie to her. "Mireille and Graziella were with us."

"Yes." She laughed faintly to herself. "Were they charming?"

"Oh, yes."

"Just as charming as ever?"

"Definitely."

"Good," her chin went up a degree, "you had a miserable time, good."

"Yes, we did."

"You deserved it."

This was by far the most intimate conversation Liliane and I had had since our marriage came apart.

We began to walk together along the beach promenade. The mistral had stopped its blast the evening before, and today there was a brisk, clear, shifting wind, ruffling the water into a blue and silver changeability. The white hotels sparkled back at the sea, the palms sparkled, old battered trucks delivering flowers sparkled, and so did the people, their hair and eyes and colored fingernails and tanned feet in sandals. A very young couple passed us, the girl angelically lovely, tanned and formed for love, the boy like a nearly naked matador.

I looked at them. They were perfect, and perfect together; they were not going to treat each other very well for very long, or even care for each other, or belong to each other or sustain anything; it was just for now or just for a while. I was convinced of that.

Liliane and I kept walking. Well out on the sea a line of sails, as white and upright as nuns, progressed slowly toward the west. An open café beside the water was playing its radio, loudly of course, like all radios and everything else here, the popular song of the summer:

7

It's your mouth that gives me my joy in living,
And my luck is to live only for you.
What do I care if you love me less . . .

How will I get rid of her, I thought to myself, How will I get rid of her? By the middle of the afternoon the heat of the sun was pouring down with an even, implacable strength. Lili and I were lying on white mattresses side by side on the beach.

She looked fresh, tanned and lithe, like a fragile Indian, black curls ruffling in the sea breeze. She had been here ten days; in other words it had taken her almost three weeks to find me. Ten days were enough to bring her beauty to its height.

"Nicholas," she said in the almost flat but at the same time emotional voice she had, a sort of tremolo flatness, as though she were constantly saying, "I don't mean to alarm you but would you mind listening to this matter of life and death," in that voice Lili said, "I'm wasting day after day here. My practicing—"

"Can't you ever take a vacation? Do you have to practice every day, even here?"

"My hands don't take a vacation, you know. My fingers begin to feel thick in forty-eight hours. Less."

"You might go back to Paris. You've got a piano at home. I bought you a piano."

"I know you did," she said. "I know you did."

"Nick!" a nasal, resonant, slightly surprised Philadelphia voice interrupted us. "I've got so much to tell you! Hello there, Liliane. Is this mattress taken? It looks clean enough. I'll just sit here and see what happens. How do you like my new beach towel?" He waved a very large towel, dull gold in color, with a large black monogram worked into it.

"Let me see that initial," Liliane said. He displayed it with a smirk. *J*.

"The Empress Josephine?" she asked.

"It's me!" he said in delight and reproach. "Jimmy."

"But that coat of arms surrounding it," she continued, "is that yours too?"

"That I just borrowed. They lent it to me at the shop. It's the coat of arms of Juan-les-Pins, I think."

"Lovely."

"Do you like it?"

"Lovely."

"Do you like it, Nick?"

"Yes, it's fine."

"Why don't you have some made yourself? Not like mine, you wouldn't want the *J*, for instance, and in some other color. Don't you think this is an attractive combination though—burnished gold and midnight? I picked out the colors myself. First I had gold and red, but that turned out to be too much. It was bad taste, Nick, bad taste. They changed it for me. It was pretty expensive because they had the red already done. But I think this has so much more style, don't you think?"

"Did they make it at that terribly expensive place beyond Pam-Pam?" Liliane asked.

Jimmy nodded with some enthusiasm. Spending surprisingly large sums of money, preferably for small and extraneous things, always elated him.

"How much was that towel," I asked, "alterations in color and all?"

"Around twenty dollars. But it will wear, you can feel that. Here, feel it. You see?"

Sergio, making his midafternoon promenade and scouting expedition, came along the sand. He nodded to Lili and me and was about to pass on when he noticed first the towel, and then Jimmy. He came over and offered us all a brief French handclasp. "Sergio," I said, "Jimmy."

"Enchanted," said Sergio brightly. "You do not speak French?"

"*Un peu,*" replied Jimmy.

At that, Sergio could be seen summoning the plainly necessary energy to speak English to this millionaire.

"You are having a fine time in Juan-les-Pins? I have noticed you having a fine time in the cabarets, I believe."

"You know what I say, Nick. Tell your friend what I always say."

"Why don't you tell him?" I said.

"Tell him, go on."

I turned to Sergio. "He says that he's living in a fever of joy."

" 'Living in a' . . . ?"

"*Fièvre de joie.*"

"That's a little exaggerated, isn't it?" commented Sergio, frowning. "You are not doing excesses, are you?"

"No!" exclaimed Jimmy, flushing and grinning uncontrollably. "But I wouldn't mind trying!"

"Your friend is *very* sympathetic," Sergio said expansively. Then to Jimmy, "You are just what we like; you bring to us some enthusiasm from America. He is nice," he nodded a proud Latin affirmative, clapping Jimmy on the back, "spontaneous!"

The thrilled surprise drained out of Jimmy's face, and he became grave with happiness. "Do you want to take a ride in my car?" he asked humbly. "It's a Porsche."

"Of course I do. I must get back to our restaurant—you don't come there, why do you never come there?—but later there will be time for a ride. . . ." and they walked off together.

"Good heavens," said Liliane mildly. "*They* aren't going to have a romance, are they?"

"No. There's just going to be an affair between Sergio and the car."

"Oh. Well, that's better." A sun-vibrant pause followed; Liliane drummed her fingers in the sand and then murmured, "I'm wasting time here."

|||||||||||||||||||||

Late afternoon seemed later and longer at Juan-les-Pins than at other places. The town after all had been created to profit from the sun, and it was as though the sun in cooperation tarried there, staying longer and shining more brightly than anywhere else. Three-quarters of the way toward the western horizon it seemed to stop, to hang there blazing, pouring warmth from that distance and angle like a hypnotist fixing his spell on his victim, to last. It broke in waves of heat over us. The afternoon hung it seemed for hours in hot decline, and the people on the beach slowly degenerated into a rabble, stunned, restless to be out of the sun but held there, fused to the sand. It was one of the two most crucial times of day in Juan-les-Pins—the other was very late at night—when people began to wonder whether they were doing the right thing. Liliane had just been a little ahead of schedule when she worried about her hands.

I got up; so did Lili, and we went down the beach, past the Café Victory. It was nearly empty at this hour, but that didn't deflate Sergio. He could be seen darting among the tables putting things here and there, snapping his towel, sniffing, speaking curtly to his mother at the cash register, dropping glasses, and sprinting into the kitchen and stamping up and down the walk in front, sweating freely in the broiling afternoon sun, wringing out the little restaurant, in case new feats of exertion might perhaps yield another five francs from it somewhere.

We walked on, coming at the end of the promenade to a little park called The Pines. It was obvious that Juan-les-Pins had once been crowded with these trees, the Mediterranean umbrella pine. But since then apartments like alternating layers of glass cut some down, cabarets and villas flattened others, widened roads and more beach and additional tennis courts struck like blights, and the surviving groves could be found only in a few marooned preserves like this little park. Lili sat down on a wrought-iron bench under one survivor in the dust and said, "Are you having dinner with me to-night?"

"No."

"What are you going to do after dinner? The girls from Antibes?"

"No, not that."

"Will you have coffee with me then?"

"All right."

"Very nice of you."

"I didn't ask you to come here."

"I know, I know."

"Well, then, you know. You recall the last time we had dinner together, don't you?" She didn't say anything. We both thought about that meal.

Finally she said, "I was happy—"

"Happy." I rubbed my foot against the gravel, vaguely noticing that it was beginning to hurt. Then I said: "You were happy with some of my friends while I was away, and you were happy with some old friends of yours who called you up, and you were happy with some stranger you ran into on the street or in a bus or God knows where. You had a lot of happiness, if that's the new word for it."

"I was happy with you," she went on, "but—"

"But what!"

"But . . . afraid."

"What were you afraid of?" I said in a voice that rasped at the edges.

She sat still for some time. Then she said in a discovering voice: "I think I was afraid of myself. Yes, I think that was it. I was afraid of some kind of—of fire there is inside me. It's been burning me for a long time. Some of it goes into my music, and that's why I play as well as I do. But there is more, much more, and it burns me, it burns me." She turned to look at me. "I was afraid of it."

"You weren't satisfied with me," I said in a metallic tone, "that's what you mean."

"No, that's not what I mean. None of—none of the"—forcing herself on—"the other people meant anything to me as you did. I was always very—very happy with you. Couldn't you feel that!" She looked at me. "Couldn't you, is it possible?"

I looked down at my foot grinding itself against the gravel. Finally I said, "I felt it."

Her shoulders seemed to lose some of their tension.

"But you had more fire," I said coldly, "more."

"Because there was something you were witholding from me! It wasn't pleasure or desire or even love. But what was it?" Her hands trembled in her lap. "Can't you tell me? I'm suffering—I—what was it? Can't you tell me, don't you know, couldn't you feel it?"

I stopped grinding my foot. "No," I said, "I gave you everything there was."

After a while she said dully, "Then it was me."

||||||||||||||||||||||

Evening faded into Juan-les-Pins like a beautiful woman making her way inconspicuously into a party. The disharmonies of the late afternoon drifted away, quietly fading into the deep night blue of the evening sky. That late-afternoon breeze that had helped stir up our argument fell now at dusk. There were a silence and a stillness, but vibrant and scintillating, because everything silent and still was so just for the moment, suspended only until the nighttime vitality began to gather itself together in Juan-les-Pins.

The new apartments, like yellow slabs of plaster and glass cutting solidly up above the pines, were full of nervous people, sold out, all rooms occupied because this was the hour of changing daylight and changing clothes. My apartment was back from the beach where the land rose a little; it was on the seventh and top floor of a building, so that I could overlook all the rest.

Juan-les-Pins was still piny from here. Sparse though they were on the ground, the trees from above fanned into full and now motionless expanses over the town. We lucky people on top floors floated up there on this sea of pine needles, and beyond the pines we saw the true sea, at this hour heavily, medievally blue, and curving into it like a dark fortification extended Cap d'Antibes, where lights began to sparkle in the darkening blue evening with pure sparkle, clear, innocent, pure sparkle.

My living room had two glass doors, "French windows" as they were called outside France, opening on a balcony two feet deep at the most, and beneath and beyond spread all this sea of green pine and Mediterranean blue with these star-like points of sparkle in the distance.

As I changed for the evening I didn't turn on any lights, so that I moved in a blue-gray glow of twilight, in the silence and stillness of this part of the day, up there above it all, sailing toward the dark coming at me across the Mediterranean sky.

Soon it was very dark. The pines deepened the darkness at Juan-les-Pins, and the core of light around the gambling casino and the shooting gallery and the always-open shops and night clubs made the surrounding piny streets seem even darker.

Down the Avenue of the Springtime, in front of my apartment house, a car shot toward this central brilliance; then its brakes screamed and screamed and at last there was an unbelievable, chaotically expanding crash. Then stillness. Soon a hoarse voice cried something, a shrill voice joined it, someone ran along the sidewalk, other cars murmured toward the scene. A little later the police wagon arrived, its horn going hee-haw hee-haw down the Avenue of the Springtime. I could see nothing from the window except beams from headlights and searchlights filtering up through the pines.

The buzzer at the door sounded loudly. The door was a very solid slab of tan wood. I opened it. Sergio and another young man smiled widely at me for a second on the threshold in the hall light and then were engulfed in blackness. The light had gone out. It worked for only three minutes at a time.

"Come in," I said into the dark, "you should have pushed the light button again."

They stumbled inside. "What's happened in the street? I heard a tremendous noise—"

"Some great racing driver, as he thinks," said Sergio imperturbably, "was doing a little practice on your street, at a hundred fifty an hour. In a beautiful Ferrari. It's unrecognizable now."

"It looks like a Renault Four-Horse now," said the other one in a soft voice and with a masked smile.

"Is the driver dead?"

Sergio had spotted my cigarettes; with a little bow and a nod and a murmured "May I?" he pulled one, two, out of the pack. "I don't think so," he then replied abstractly, with the cigarette in his mouth and his eye squinting from the smoking match.

"What did he hit?"

"Another car. A parked car. Truly a great racing driver. Champion."

"Then I suppose the Season is open at Juan-les-Pins. A Ferrari has been broken up in the street."

"Evidently."

"Thank God," murmured the other one.

The remark recalled to Sergio the other's existence. "This is Jeannot," he said with an Italian open-handed gesture toward him. Jeannot moved across to me with a certain controlled grace, like a self-possessed cat; we grasped hands, and he murmured, "Enchanted, Monsieur." He was very dark, with a fine-looking face in an unexpected way.

"Why do you say 'Thank God'?" Sergio continued.

"Thank God that the Season has begun," Jeannot replied in his quiet voice. His black eyes moved quickly from one of us to the other, "even with a car accident, it is not amusing, Juan-les-Pins out of season. No work, you know?"

"Ah, yes," said Sergio, still in reverie, "I know." Then his eyes, which had become large, dreaming, younger in their expression, as we talked, now slowly and almost reluctantly focused and narrowed into their habitual sharpness. "You wished to change twenty dollars, wasn't it? Good. They are now paying 485 francs to the dollar. Not bad, no? Considering that the official rate is 420."

"Not bad," I agreed.

Jeannot, who seemed to be a responsive type of person, nodded quickly.

As Sergio handed me the beautiful French bills and I handed him my business-like traveler's check he said: "We do not accept these checks from everyone, naturally. Only from the people we know, good guys, like you. Others change the checks with us and then report them to the company. The company gives them new

15

checks and stops payment on the others. So they have robbed us. Real sons of bitches. Well, after all, there are racketeers everywhere."

Jeannot and I both concurred again.

"And now our other business," he continued.

"Other business?"

"Yes, you mentioned the other day that your typewriter—the machine you use for those mysterious reports you make to America" —he grinned with pleased complicity; Sergio, whose mind worked that way, thought I was a spy—"you mentioned that it is working badly."

"Yes, as a matter of fact that's true. I'd forgotten about that."

"Well, I didn't forget. My Jeannot here is a typewriter repairman of the first class. Aren't you?"

Jeannot nodded again, with a flash of eagerness on his dark face.

It was on the floor behind a table. Jeannot went over and picked it up. On the table was a little glass jug with a few cut geraniums in it. They had been there for some time, many days, more than a week, perhaps two weeks, and they had gone on and on being bright and alive-looking, optimistic, as fresh as music. They had gone on for so long that I had begun to ask myself almost seriously whether flowers weren't somehow immortal in the South of France.

Jeannot set the typewriter on the table and began to tinker. I noticed that he was really going to be able to fix it by the way his elbows were bent, or in the inclination of his head over the keys, or perhaps in the hunching of his shoulders. Something. He knew what he was doing; it was written all over the way he held himself. With his black hair hovering over my old typewriter, he made little tapping noises and tentative clicks on the keys, and then reached inside and touched something, or turned something else with a tiny tool.

A few minutes later he tested it with a typed sentence. I went over to see how it worked. AM A POOR UNFORTUNATE LOOKING FOR WORK was neatly spelled across the piece of yellow paper in capital letters. His head bent a little lower. "I didn't know you were going to read it," he mumbled. "I wanted to see if it would work."

Sergio's sharp nose pointed at the paper. "It works well, you see? He does good work, no?"

"*He's* very good, but your contribution—"

"I know the customers," Sergio cut in good-humoredly, "I know the business. And of course I know the proper prices. For you, naturally, I am not going to charge the usual tourist price, 2,000 francs, and certainly not the *American* tourist price—"

"How much is that?"

"Three thousand francs," he answered automatically. "I am not charging even the regular French price, 1,500 francs. No, my dear Nicholas, not even the *friend's* price, 1,000 francs. For you I will charge only the *family* price, 500 francs. We are like brothers, Nicholas and I," he added proudly to Jeannot.

It seemed very reasonable, just a little more than one of Sergio's black-market dollars. I suspected that Sergio would keep the dollar and give Jeannot what remained.

Jeannot crossed the room toward the door. He had on a pair of strong leather sandals, shiny and seasoned leather, old and tough and shiny. They were timeless Mediterranean sandals, Appian Way sandals. He was very dark, South Italian or Spanish perhaps, except that he spoke French without an accent. Probably an Arab, then, who had gone to a French elementary school. I gave Sergio the 500 francs, we all shook hands, Sergio flashing his quick, confidential smile, Jeannot a more tentative one, and they left. Another poor unfortunate looking for work.

I dressed carefully for the night in Juan-les-Pins. Thin, pliable leather loafers, white. A pair of shiny sky-blue slacks, with narrow legs and a band instead of a belt at the waist. A lighter blue shirt of firm cloth, open to below the chest, collar standing up around my neck. In other words, as ordinary as possible. Dressed like that, no one would pay any attention to me at Juan-les-Pins.

I took the elevator, which wasn't out of order this evening, to the ground floor and walked out into the burnt musky smell of Juan-les-Pins in the evening. Noise from the center of town reverberated like the sound of a distant football game. I set out toward it along the peaceful streets.

There were three people at the corner talking in carefully controlled voices, two policemen and a dark, ragged youth, an Algerian probably, but not the one who had fixed my typewriter. Something about papers, documents. The Algerian's weren't in order; in the dark I couldn't see his face, but his voice was as controlled as theirs.

I turned into the Boulevard of the President Wilson. Three blocks farther the boulevard came to an end at Pam-Pam.

Everyone was there. Pam-Pam was lighted like an operating room, so it was easy to see everyone. Max, in his blazing hair and shrieking pants, sat in the little cluttered open bar at the back of the terrace, laughing at something Mireille had said. She glared furiously back at him. Jimmy Smoot was established on the terrace with a plain girl. The jukebox was broadcasting a pulsing cha-cha-cha.

As I moved slowly past with the crowd I suddenly felt an out-of-sight commotion. Behind the blocking shoulders and heads something had scared the crowd. It felt like the blind start of a riot. Then the people broke; a bicycle careened toward the café; it was going to hit the first table, but, twirling, it hurtled back across the street. On it a man with a huge cigar was busily playing the fiddle. He had on shorts and a beach shirt and a funny hat. He careened toward a car coming very slowly along, flung up his front wheel, grazing the bumper, and then turned into the crowd; people sprang giggling out of the way. He rode backward, he rode the handlebars, he nearly collided with a dozen people and cars. As a climax he wriggled the bike miraculously through the jammed terrace of Pam-Pam without touching any of the furniture or any of the customers.

A woman came toward me as I made my way along Azure Street. She was accompanied by four feral dogs, their leashes and yelps entangled. The woman was not aware of their confusion. She was turning her big flour-white face to the right and left, making cordial greetings. Her large eyes slid in their sockets this way and that, and her hands holding the leashes were clasped graciously at her waist. She was a large woman, and on her feet she wore large tennis shoes. As she went past me she gave her greeting to an invisible person beside me, but although she was speaking she made no sound. From behind, her straw red-black hair formed a rigid pyramid, and her shoulders were big and square, like a man's. Her head continued to turn to the right and left, giving her placating greeting to space.

I found the restaurant I was looking for, blue and dark red, with a table full of fruit and pastries and flowers in the center. I ordered a hard-boiled egg with mayonnaise, a few sardines, a small steak with béarnaise sauce, some round, browned potatoes, a salad in which every leaf had been given its own shower of olive oil and vinegar and garlic, cheese which gave under the knife, and a pastry that burst and fulfilled itself when the fork broke into it. With this I had French bread, and a half-bottle of red wine—not any red wine, but Pommard, which always reached depths of taste I possessed but had never known about before.

I looked over a newspaper for temporary company. Sporadic pro-De Gaulle demonstrations on the Champs-Elysées.

Two street entertainers came by, truly Mediterranean, that is, middle-aged, wearing worn dark suits, failures, a little desperate. They were Italians; one played the accordion and the other was a tenor. The tenor's face was sad, the accordionist looked as if he suffered from high blood pressure. They began. Out of the trapped accordion surged some Neapolitan gaiety, some bouncing song from the streets. The tenor began singing, a voice full of energy, as though from some independent store of energy he had available to his voice alone. It was all music, his voice clear and exuberant and natural. People talked through his singing, but they noticed when he stopped, and applauded. The Italians looked a little better. Then they offered a great favorite:

> *As before,*
> *You give me so much joy*
> *That no one else gives me.*
> *It's your mouth. . . .*

This time more people paid attention, and there was a little more applause. The tenor leaned over a table to hear a request. His voice wasn't his only natural gift; he had also been given natural grace, he leaned with instinctive knowledge, a diplomat's bow. The waiting accordionist released a random, lively flight. The request was a bouncy, rapping, hot-cha song, spoofing and cheerful and slap-happy, but it had a natural Mediterranean orderliness too. This time most people broke off their conversations to listen, and everybody applauded. The two Italians collected their money—both of them had the bows of diplomats—and then they moved on, looking younger.

I paid for the dinner and walked back down Azure Street toward the Victory. In front of me a photographer danced backward, aiming his camera. I put an expression on my face, his bulb flared; then he made a short bow and handed me a card, the address of a shop where I could pick up the picture in the morning. He bobbed off toward an elderly English couple. At Juan-les-Pins flash bulbs were going off at you and around you all the time; every night had the kind of hurried, meager glamour of a movie opening. We were all stars here, or at least promising juveniles and starlets.

The Café Victory wasn't as crowded as Pam-Pam. There was more space between the tables, and the three-piece orchestra wasn't very noisy. Pam-Pam faced the intersection and other cafés, but the Victory looked out on the sea. Lili was at a table on the terrace, trying to look alone. But a stocky, gypsy-like youth leaned across the table, his eyes working.

"How was your dinner?" she said as I came up, "this is—well, I don't know who this is."

The gypsy became the soul of deference before he had even fully looked at me, rose, shook hands formally, eyes down, and said, "Monsieur's friend has permitted me a moment's conversation. Good promenade, and good evening," and he smoothly faded into the café.

"You can't even sit alone here," Lili said lightly. "I suppose it's flattering."

"And you like that."

"All women—"

"But not the way you do."

"Nick, why not just have coffee pleasantly together. Why argue?"

"What the hell else is there for us to do? Why did you come here anyway? What are you doing on the Riviera?"

"I'm trying to continue being your wife."

Something shot to my brain, the Pommard or the stab of memory, and I said rapidly, with rattled lightness, "Why do you need me! Let *me* go! You've got strings of replacements!"

"Please stop, please."

"I'm embarrassing you in *public*."

She kept her eyes shut until whatever she was feeling wouldn't show in them, and then she looked at me. "If I caused you to—to lose control of yourself, your equilibrium," she began quietly, "then I'm the one to—repair, to make it up."

But I was having none of that, none at all, not now or ever. "I think that you're about the last person," I said steadily, "who can do anything good for me." I watched her head go down, and sat looking at her black and shiny hair.

After a while she brought her head up, and I could see that she was struggling no longer with me but with herself. She took a deep breath, and on her face there was a listening expression. She seemed to be trying to find out how much damage had been done to her. I saw this and didn't care at all, felt no trace of pity, was glad of it. Good. She had broken me, not my "heart," that romantic myth; there is no "heart" in the emotions. She had broken my mind, specifically and physically an organ, *the* organ of the body. She had broken that. I watched her assess her own injuries.

And then, on the surface anyhow, Liliane was all right again. Personality reentered her eyes and filtered across her face. It was pure instinctual strength and control that enabled this to happen. Probably she really was the great musician she and others believed her potentially to be; I didn't know enough about music to know.

But there it was, this reserve of personal strength. There it was, pulling her back. If I myself had had it . . .

"We've been invited to a party tonight on Cap d'Antibes," she said with a pleasant expression on her delicate face. "Some friends of mine—you've never met them—have a villa there. Would you like to go? Please. Do this for me. I know you don't want to. But if you would just do this for me tonight. Will you?"

"Why do you want me to?"

"I—I want you to. I don't know, please. We're going to separate —we are separated—but I can't go there alone tonight. Won't you do this for me?"

"There's no point in it."

"You've got to help me," she said abruptly in a strange voice.

I was shaken by the tone and by something in her face. "All right," I said casually, "yes, I'll go."

My car was parked on a nearby sidewalk, illegally. So far the police hadn't bothered it. They were probably too busy arresting Algerians. As I drove the car off the sidewalk, Liliane said, "There's always some disturbance in France."

We drove very slowly through the clogged Pam-Pam inter-section, past the Casino where an elegant couple were getting out of a monarchical car, and then we crossed the invisible circumference of Juan-les-Pins night life; suddenly it was very dark, and there was no one.

Along the edge of the sea the road curved between carefully made stone walls. "Who are these friends of yours?" I asked.

"They are brother and sister, Marc de la Croie, and Constance —Madame Courcelles. And there are several children of hers, or at least one."

"Won't the children be in bed? Or do they stay up all night too on the Riviera?"

"Well, they're not what you would call children, I suppose. They're about twenty or twenty-two."

Light and shadows from the moon-shining sea flowed over Lili's face. I turned a little and saw her eyes from the side. She was looking ahead, so that I could not see into them, but they revealed nothing when I looked into them anyway. They revealed something only from this very oblique angle, where I could hardly see them at all. Liliane's eyebrows curved more fully and the eyes were set in more deeply than I remembered.

"I didn't mention to them that I had gotten married," she said. "I didn't see the point of it, under the circumstances."

"I see."

We rounded a curve, carved out of the front of the home of Mr. Jack L. Warner; its name was printed on the front, the Castle of Today, and it was built flush with, was in fact a part of, the road's curve. We turned another curve, climbing, a rock with a ruined tower above us, the sea, endlessly dark and shiny and deep, mingling with the rocks below—fifty years ago it must all have been very beautiful—drove past the ducal gates of the Hôtel du Cap d'Antibes, a fragile château in the moonlight, and then we turned into a white lane between low chiseled walls, and came to a Mediterranean house.

My car was a very small, dark-blue, very fast Alfa-Romeo two-seater—it was like driving a bullet. When I turned off the engine we dropped into an unnatural, clinging silence. It was as though there had never been any noise here. We walked across the gravel, making expensive sounds with our shoes, and went into the house through the open door. "Have you been here before?" I asked.

"Yes, but not lately. Everyone must be on the terrace."

"Leaving the door wide open. Somebody could steal all their jewels."

Even crime was graceful on the Riviera; it always broke out because of passion, ideology, or jewels.

As we crossed the hall and a large living room, I had the impression of being in the priory of a prospering, lax, and civilized religious order; dark ceiling beams, dark carved furniture, tile floor, Roman arches, flares of Southern color on the walls and couches, flowers and space and soft yellow lamplight.

A woman appeared at the doorway of the terrace. Her face was not out of place in this atmosphere of indulgent religion. She looked like a worldly saint: an aura of wavy dark-brown hair, expectant blue eyes, and a tolerant mouth. Her dress was blue and crisp and costly, and a few jewels—a ring, a pin, a necklace—shone against her tan. This was Constance. She spoke in English, and her voice sounded as though she had always had and always enjoyed everything. As she came across to us I noticed that she was enjoying being a little drunk.

"We're all out here," she said with a short, irresponsible laugh, adding as she led us out, "Pay no attention to any conversation about politics."

On the terrace five people were talking in a mingling of light from the house and light from the moon. All of them were older than ourselves except for Constance's son, who was in his early twenties and who was introduced to me as "Titou."

"Cute, isn't it?" he said in easy but thick English. "My name is actually Victor. About 1940 all the family found Victor a bit too ironic, too grotesque as a word—they couldn't endure hearing it around the house—so they adopted my own way of pronouncing it. One of these days France is going to win a war somewhere, and then I will be allowed to grow up." He was a little drunk too, not indulgently like his mother, but excitably drunk, which made his small-boned, heavy-lidded, sensual French face seem even cleverer. "You don't care about France in 1940, do you?" and he grinned with hazy affection at me and winked enormously at Liliane.

"Not politics, I beg you," said Constance with a trace of mock piteousness as she handed Lili and me a glass of something and then drifted off.

"De Gaulle to power! We're all agreeing on that subject tonight," Titou raced on. "In 1940 they all agreed on Pétain to power. We do agree now and then in France. We were all Pétainists in 1940, of course. I was too young to do very much agreeing, as a matter of fact. But I would have been a Pétainist, as all my family was. My Uncle Marc only was a little slow; he kept being a Pétainist in 1941,

24

in 1942, in 1943, in 1944. . . . He has the worst sense of timing in the family. Can't even dance. Hopeless. A Pétainist, in 1944!" He raised his glass in a toast, and we tasted our drinks. Scotch. "Let's go sit on the wall."

"I thought Marc danced very well," Lili murmured as we crossed to a low wall.

Titou crowed with surprised laughter, and I thought I saw a flicker of embarrassment in her eyes for once. "I don't know what the reason for that rather silly laughter was. Unless it is that you seem to have been drinking—"

"Scotch! I love Scotch. I loathed Scotland—they sent me for a summer in Scotland once to learn English—my whole family is mad—but I adore Scotch. De Gaulle to power!"

We sat down on the low wall. I happened to look behind it. Space and blackness, with a few ridges of cliff far below gilded by the moonlight, and the sea muttering in the void at the bottom.

"Now I am going to tell you all about Pétain." He patted Lili's hands clenched in her lap, and they dutifully relaxed. She returned his low-lidded, conspiratorial, frank and flirting grin with a charming smile, like a very affectionate sister's, no speck of embarrassment left. Then he squeezed my arm. "Look at my Uncle Marc. No, over there." I looked. "Not stupid-looking, wouldn't you agree? But he wouldn't get away from Pétain until much too late, and so everybody put him in jail, the Germans, the Gaullists, everybody."

"You know he's been completely cleared of all that," said Liliane tersely, "and it's not a thing to discuss at a party in front of guests!"

"Oh," Titou's head shook impatiently from side to side, a metronome. "Little French girl of good family. I want to tell your lover something."

She shrugged quietly, and Titou said, "Here is why Uncle Marc and all the family and everyone else became a Pétainist." He cocked an eye at me. "You're not French, are you?"

"My mother was French."

"What was your father? I knew you weren't French because you can't quite pronounce the letter *t* the way we do. What was your father, without indiscretion?"

"My father was a Russian."

"White Russian?"

"Yes."

"And what are you?—I am not too impolite, I trust . . . all these questions."

"No, not at all. I'm an American citizen."

"Well then . . . perhaps you were not here in 1940."

"We left in 1940."

"Then let me translate the situation the French faced in 1940 to America for you. I know America very well. Have you been to Grand Island, Nebraska?"

"No."

"I have been. I had driven across all America once. I thought it was divine. Without charm, however."

"Have you ever been to New England?"

"Very little. Has it charm? I will go when I visit America again. Now. It is 1940. We are going to put America in the place of France. America is in the war with its biggest enemy, which has just captured New York City. You are living in Albany. All right? The enemy is coming up the Hudson River, fast. Your own army has disappeared, as far as you can learn, unless it is in Canada or somewhere. The government has fled away from Washington, which your enemy has also captured, and moved to St. Louis. Then it is in Albuquerque, and now you hear that maybe it is in Seattle and going to get on a boat and sail away to somewhere. You don't care too much about them any more, because you understand that half of them have been working with the enemy from the beginning. Your only ally was Canada, and they are getting all their soldiers and every piece of equipment and everything else Canadian out of your country as fast as they can. You have another friendly country, China, but it happens to be on the other side of the world and it never does anything except to make friendly sounds and then say it wouldn't dream of becoming involved in any trouble in America ever. So there you are!

"It is the end of the United States, the end of honor, the end of everything safe, the horrible void.

"Then one day on the radio there comes the voice of your greatest military hero. He is your old pure military hero, who saved you in the earlier war and was not in any way involved in the present debacle. It is the General Pershing. He tells you that he is going to be the chief of a pure and fine American government to be put up on the trash heap of the old one, and it will rescue and uphold the traditional spirit of America. Of course you weep, with relief. And that is why Uncle Marc was a Pétainist!"

"Anybody would have been," said Liliane with certainty. "It is a shame, how he was made to suffer for just that."

Titou rolled his lidded eyes toward her. "Not quite 'just that,' my flower."

Lili looked across the terrace. "Shouldn't Nicholas meet Monsieur Marc," she said, "as long as he seems to be the subject of conversation tonight?"

Titou took my arm. "He was a Pétainist of the Pétainists, my dear uncle." We got up. "There was a question of some people in hiding—"

Lili interrupted in a level voice. "If you say another word, Titou."

He immediately nuzzled her neck, a puppy. "All right, all right, fidèle. Isn't she adorable? All the most adorable women I meet through the generosity of my uncle."

The uncle came forward and I was introduced to him. He was tall and square-shouldered and self-contained; he wore an elegant double-breasted French suit and he had humorous blue French eyes. He was very handsome in the prominent-nosed French way, longish black hair graying quietly, ruddy complexion toned with tan, a level, rolling, self-controlled and faintly musical voice. He looked straight at me when we were introduced as though this was what he had really been waiting for.

We moved toward the wall, and M. Marc lighted a cigarette. It was a Gauloise, too plebian for him, one would have thought. Its musky smell drifted into the air around us, merging with the salt air and the Maritime pines, and everything began to seem more permissible than before; a Mediterranean laxness made itself felt; the lived-in, forgetful, experienced air of the South of France in the nighttime settled languidly around us.

We were sitting on the wall again, M. Marc, then Lili, then myself, then Titou. The others across the terrace were discussing calmly, autumnally, the disappearance of French cuisine. "In ten years," one of them observed, "not so much as a trace will be left." Someone else maintained that those final ten years were already past, and a compromiser said that here and there, far from the tourist trails that had brutalized every French chef along them, there persisted a few cooks who still put their imaginations and their lives into their food, a few clients who knew what standards to insist on, and retained the independence of character and taste to insist. But there were very few such cooks and such clients, and they were aging and dying out.

M. Marc changed the subject on our part of the terrace. He didn't seem to be interested in food. "We have been discussing the Algerian trouble," he said. "It is of interest, I think. Are you comfortable sitting there? Quite bad hospitality, forcing our guests to sit on stone. You don't find it too uncomfortable? Well then.

"Yes, we have been saying that we French will have to do something decisive about Algeria soon. For one reason, the disturbances are no longer confined to Algeria. There are hundreds of thousands of Algerians here in France; they are French citizens, like—myself." There was a pause, brief as a heel click, before the last word. "They fight and kill each other here every day now. Something must be done." His cigarette hung in the side of his mouth under his full upper lip. One eye was squinting slightly from the smoke, giving him an acute look. "Their morality is Moslem, not Christian. They are far from their own towns and families and habits. They come here to work, temporarily. They are all supreme fatalists, of course. Life is as Allah wills, all of it, always.

"But lately these Arabs," he went on, "have become political criminals. In Algeria, as you know, they have a kind of haphazard band of an army that has been at war with, or rather fighting, the French Army for four years. Here in France there is also much killing."

"I didn't realize that," Liliane said in a breath.

"For the most part they have been killing each other. So not so much notice is taken; the newspapers have not been paying a great deal of attention."

"But why should they kill each other?" asked Lili.

"Because some of them are absolutely against France and some are moderates. There are disputes among the two groups. The absolute rebels get angry because the moderates will not cooperate enough, not contribute enough money to support the band of rebels who are causing all this disorder in Algeria. So they kill some moderates to frighten the others. Or else a fanatical rebel becomes too threatening and a group of moderates rise and kill him, to frighten the fanatics."

"How horrible to be an *Arab!*" she exclaimed.

"Yes."

"Don't be too, too sympathetic, *bébé*," Titou aroused himself from a Scotch haze to say; "they're beginning to bump us off now. Right here in France. Say how horrible to be French. Sympathize with me. Sit over here and give me some sympathy. I suffer mortally. How I suffer."

M. Marc was gazing at him with a steady gleam of affection; Liliane turned her beam on him for a moment, and Titou, finding that he had stumbled into the hot light, blinked his lidded eyes, sighed tragically, and smirked back at them. "I suffer in agony."

"I'm always terrified of Arabs," said Liliane thoughtfully, not exactly ignoring Titou, but pulling back to seriousness again. "Do they all carry knives?" she asked, addressing herself pretty directly to M. Marc.

"A great many do. They are subject to search by the police, so they must be on guard. Still, they have their fatalism; if they are caught it is Allah's will. That enables them to carry knives very often, and that, the fatalism, is their most dangerous weapon of all. Much worse than any knives." He tilted his head toward her and smiled slightly. "But don't worry, they would never harm you with a knife. Harm you? Never. They would take care not to harm you with their knives."

"Uncle, *s'il vous plaît!*" Titou came, comically indignant, back into the conversation. "If you're going to flirt outrageously with this guest's mistress, you'll stain the hospitality of the house!"

"Titou, don't be an imbecile," M. Marc said over the last part of this.

"I," began Titou with shaky grandeur, like a drunken little emperor, "am going to ruin the family honor and flirt with her myself, if anybody does. I am the one to plant the wild oats now. You've done yours, and we've harvested them, and eaten them when we had to"—he was getting excited with himself—"and they didn't taste too good, I can tell you. Very sour and vinegarish and rotten they were, and still we've had to have your wild oats for breakfast cereal, and wild-oat salad and wild-oat soufflé, and some wild-oat dessert sometimes, and wild-oat purges and wild-oat whisky and we're all sick—"

Lili had been hushing and then seizing and then shaking Titou harder and harder; he turned on her now. "*Lache-moi!* Another of his wild oats! That's what I mustn't say, no! Your—"

She slapped him. His face set furiously, his hand shot up to slap her; then he just stopped himself. M. Marc moved and then Constance was at Titou's elbow, with no trace of her slight tipsiness. "Have you lost your minds?" she said swiftly in French, the rich overtones still in her voice.

"Have *we!*" Lili said indignantly. "Your pig of a son—"

"Victor, leave us," Constance said, turning on him.

"I should have *left* long ago!"

"Dead drunk," M. Marc said calmly and coolly, "the boy is dead drunk." We forget what a child he still is."

"Do you want me to grow up like you?" Titou demanded.

"Enough!" M. Marc and Constance cried almost together.

"Enough, enough, enough," Titou mimicked scornfully, as with Constance prodding him he stumbled toward the house, "enough."

On the other side of the terrace, in a nerveless triumph of social tact, the others had never stopped for a moment talking about the decayed state of French food. As Titou went by them there was just a moment's suspension, and then, seeing that they were not going to be directly attacked, they recommended in the same tones: "Of course when today *rosé* is made by mixing white with red, what can you expect? Our wines are worthy of our food which, as we all know . . ."

Constance came up to us again. Her composure was total; she had the calmness of gardening. "After he has drunk a great deal of mineral water he will come back and make the apologies he wishes to make, to you Mademoiselle Liliane, to his uncle, and to our other guests. "We are not used to Anglo-Saxon whiskies. They are a fad here this year, a bad one, I should say. And Titou is over-excitable by nature." She smiled, her own nature with its indulgence beginning to return.

M. Marc gazed at Lili and me for a moment with eyes warm with something, pride of self-love or courage or ancestry. Then he smiled a little, a knit French smile, and inclining his head an inch he said in his well-placed voice, "I am sorry." He continued to look at us for a moment, eyes warm and speculative, and then the scene was over.

"If the Arabs," began Liliane uncertainly, "weren't so uneducated, perhaps . . ."

"We spawned them ourselves, with some of our French ideas of equality and so on, we made them intoxicated. That was half the reason for the present rebellion. The other half was French medicine. We saved lives, so many lives, all these Arab lives we saved.

Most of the babies live instead of die in Algeria now, and have done, thanks to us, for many years. By force of numbers they are now crowding us out of the country. French medicine, French education. Because of these two gifts the giver is being driven out. It does not seem entirely just."

"No," said Liliane, pondering.

"We should now take back these gifts," he continued. "It is necessary. We shall lose everything unless we strike at the true sources of the problem. Pacification will not do. We must close our schools and stop all our medical assistance. It is not impossible. It is almost certainly too late, but it must be attempted, or else we should surrender altogether, give them their independence, and save our French lives and money. We shall need both in the pitiable future for France that will ensue, once we have lost Algeria.

"No, the single solution is to take back our gifts of education and medicine. Those Arabs who then wish to leave the country would be permitted to do so, with the greatest pleasure on our part. The Arab world is vast. They would be free to immigrate to their fellow Arab sympathizers, to Tunisia or Morocco or Egypt. There they would be able to discover what kind of education and medical treatment are available to them in these *independent* countries; they would learn just how much they have been indebted to France all these many years. Let them go to these countries.

"Once they are gone we can recommence our education and health measures. Those who remain would be absorbed and mingled with the million French, Italian, and other European elements of the population in Algeria. More French would be encouraged to migrate there. The country would cease after a time to be Arab and Moslem. It would become European and Christian. In that way it would be truly joined to France. The present 'merger' of Algeria and France, pretending that they are merely a part of the same whole, is a fiction, as everyone knows. One cannot merge wine and hashish. The country will be made French when its inhabitants are overwhelmingly French and Christian. There is nothing in the land itself, after all, that forbids it. Regard North America, for example. It was once pagan and Indian, and now it is Christian and Anglo-Saxon. So there is this precedent in America for what I am saying. I believe what I suggest would be more humane and reasonable than the seizure from the Indians of that beautiful country."

On top of a hill behind and above us was a lighthouse that sent a diffused path of brightness now and then slowly overhead across the sky. Well out from the shore naval ships were anchored, dark hulks, but startlingly, frivolously festooned with lights forming gay triangles on their rigging, bright and lively as circuses, formidable and playful at the same time. Far beyond them the South Coast of France curved back into the sea with bits of light scattered over its blackness like the particles of phosphorus the sea leaves behind on the shore.

"The Côte d'Azur is ruined," M. Marc said after the silence. It was typical of my relationship to him—it was already so firmly set in my mind that it had its particular characteristics—that he would have said exactly the reverse of what I was thinking. The Côte d'Azur was not ruined. No one had changed the inspired color of the sea yet; no one had shut off the sun; the flowers grew as before; the air kept on making long lives longer. The Côte d'Azur was not ruined, although there were many such people who said it was. "It is this program of the governments," he went on, "paid vacations, which is ruining it. All the workers coming here with their families and their tents—no one begrudges them their holiday in the sun of course," a genial smile, "but the Riviera is like a small and beautiful château; you destroy it if the occupants become a crowd."

People who complain that the Riviera is ruined, I said to myself bitterly, are talking about themselves. They're the ruins. They've had so much of so many good things that they have to compare and disparage and discriminate, just to differentiate what they are getting this time from what they got the last. The palms and pines in the garden, silent and sculptured against the black and shining sky, seemed on my side in this argument, this silent argument; I knew in advance that Liliane would be on his side, and so I kept quiet. The three of us sat without speaking, in the midst of the loveliest ruin in the world, and watched the phosphorescent lights of the long coast line burning on against the sky.

Titou came back onto the terrace. He walked slowly toward us, tripped, then stood in front of us, giving an impression somehow of an infant after its nap, an impression of warmth and moisture and half-consciousness, and he said in a heartfelt murmur, "I'm sorry," smiling timidly. "You'll forgive me?"

M. Marc gazed at him with his half-smile, his eyes glowing, and said, "But of course," very cordially and confidently. "Here, sit here. Tell Liliane about my sins—"

"No, no," Titou protested tremulously.

"We must go," Lili said, "Nick and I. We've stayed and stayed because it is so lovely here. But we must go. I want to see a little of the cabarets here—*he* has seen it already, of course."

"I can imagine!" exclaimed Titou, rolling his eyes, completely recovered.

"Amuse yourselves well," said M. Marc, giving my hand a shake, "and come again very soon. We don't often have a chance to discuss the world with young people who know it so well."

"O-o-o," Titou crowed, "they're worldly, worldly!" and he gave my hand a single shake too.

We crossed the terrace to thank Constance, and all three of them walked through the house with us to the car. Constance took my hand there as I thanked her again, and held it, not grasping but really letting her own hand rest in it, and said pleasantly: "You will come again? With Liliane, or not, as it happens. We are almost always at home at this time. With the others here I hadn't a moment to—"

"Good night, Constance," said Lili, getting into the car on the other side.

"Good night," Constance said, withdrawing her hand, gazing across with a cordial smile at Lili.

We drove back through the white lane, pale and dry and crackling under our wheels in the moonlight.

"That's a corrupt family," said Liliane suddenly.

"What made you say that?"

"I've been thinking it from time to time all evening. It appears sooner or later if you spend any time with them. I'll not take you there again. Not that you need *me* to take you there after tonight! Now that you've made your conquest of Constance."

"Conquest! I hardly said ten words to her."

"I know her. I've seen that look on her face before. You knew you'd made a success with her."

"No, I didn't know that, to tell the truth."

"Oh, yes, you knew." She seemed to be saying this more to herself than to me, reassuring herself that by bringing it up she hadn't helped it along, hadn't set a match to something that might not have combusted spontaneously, hadn't spilled the beans. The thought had just barely occurred to me, just touched my mind as Constance's hand stayed in mine at the car, and then I'd forgotten it.

"Speaking of that family's love affairs, you and Monsieur Marc were, at least at one time—close. . . ." Out, by God! I didn't even know I was going to say it, but everybody seemed to say everything tonight, and so my mind had been building up somewhere, working itself under cover up to *its* liberation, storing confidence from M. Marc's exposure on Algeria, from Titou's on M. Marc, from Lili's on Constance, from Constance's seeming flirting with me, biding its time and finally, because my mind had accumulated all this strength without letting me know it, becoming too strong for my control, seizing my voice and putting my suspicion, my accusation out there in front of her face. "That," I went on, my voice firm and confident from the relief of it, "was what Titou was driving at all night. Why did you take me with you? To impress me with another of your lovers? Was that it?"

"They're a strange family," she said quietly. "I told you that. I'm . . . afraid of them. I was afraid to go there tonight alone."

"You and Marc—"

"Do you really want to discuss Marc and me now?"

After a pause I said, "No."

"Then let's go to Maxim's. The entertainment is a troupe of female impersonators. I've always wanted to see some."

||||||||||||||||||||

Maxim's was white and open to the sky, with thin palm trees growing among the tables, an orchestra in a shell, waiters sliding around tanned women in light dresses, a feeling of fashionable stimulation in the air. At the bar, a long shining slot of light under the palms, I saw Jimmy Smoot listening happily and nervously to some story being told to him with frowning intensity and many tight gestures by Sergio; Max lolling in his red pants on another stool next to a tall, plain, English-looking girl who interrupted gulps of her drink to try conversing with him; Mireille clutching her thin little poodle.

Liliane and I sat down at a table. "You don't mind taking me out? It's not going to ruin your reputation, is it? Being seen with your wife?"

The female impersonators came on in wigs, heightened eyes, bony arms and rasping voices, flying feathers and taut glittering dresses, mocking and loud and defiant. A big lithe dancer, in halter and shorts, threw professionally burning glances in our direction during his number. "I knew you'd make another conquest," Lili said. "Isn't he cute? Especially with that rhinestone in his navel."

We stayed for about an hour, and since the show gradually became too boring to watch and we could not find anything to say to each other, we then left. Outside, the holocaust of Juan-les-Pins blazed on, shooting galleries and clogged cafés and blaring night clubs, but walking past one, a little temporary enclosure of bamboo and straw—Juan-les-Pins was half bamboo and straw in the summer,

36

like an Asiatic colony that had floated home to France—we heard the lilting song which was everywhere then,

And my luck is to live only for you.
What do I care if you love me less . . .

and we went inside for a moment. Passing through the bamboo, we walked down a stone stairway into a sunken court below the promenade next to the beach. Against one wall was a small fountain, with a design on the tile panel behind it of a god, waves, a boat, and a fish. A little orchestra, mostly an accordion from the streets, played the kind of lively nostalgia the accordion alone can play, the kind of music people liked here.

The Provençals were dancing around us, the young men mostly in bright, tight blue pants, moccasin shoes with the pliability of dancing slippers, blue striped shirts; or severe Italian gray pants sculpturally cut, and white shirts of fine mesh. Their hair formed black helmets over hawk profiles and dark eyes burned into awareness by the sun. The girls wore dresses with the shiny festiveness of Christmas wrapping, but they themselves were usually grave, grave glowing dark eyes, slow smiles, with the slim perfect bodies of the very young girls of the Mediterranean. Some were blonde, long, long burnished blond hair falling around their faces that had been brought so alive by all the sun, and the wide-set, distilled clarity of their eyes.

The music grew livelier. It was African music that had come to France after a long sea change. The jungle drums weren't taken seriously any more; the compulsive beat was only played with, taken up, parodied, humorously dropped, taken up with mock intensity again. Nobody seemed to be drinking very much; nobody was going to be seized with a dancing frenzy and nobody was going to pass out. The balance of Provence: there were no wild Northern visions to be released, and no jungle frenzies either. The music expressed it: the syncopation, the beat, the rattle, with the melody lilting and soaring above; then the music changed, charged, there was a beat skipped, a mocking rattle again, the drums urged excitement, and over and through it all there was the sweet, orderly, heartbroken lilt of a French song.

We danced—there are many different rituals for saying good-bye—and Liliane's shining dress slid under my hand. Her hair, smelling faintly of the sea wind, touched my face. I remembered how slim she was. We didn't say anything to each other.

When we left to walk along the promenade, the Mediterranean was rolling a miniature surf of little silver curving waves against the beach, one after another, carefully made waves coming carefully in to break all at once with a miniature crash against the sand.

We turned up a dark street and walked under the trees of roses with their odors promising us—anything, promising us happiness everlasting, if only we had known where to look for it, if only we had started yesterday or waited until tomorrow, if only we had found the key—it was everywhere, like the odor itself—there were keys everywhere, all around us, but so many that we had become confused and not found one; the keys were everywhere, and the happiness they unlocked was supreme and everlasting, but we had not looked in the right place at the right time, that was all.

||||||||||||||||||||

The next day I had to make a short visit to San Remo, just across the frontier in Italy, to see a man about some leather. I drove quickly along between the translucent sea and the hills sparkling in the sunshine, into mock-monarchical Nice and on through Ville-franche and past Cap Ferrat, up and into and out of the operetta setting of Monte Carlo, into Italianate Menton, and finally on a hill with leftover gun emplacements commanding the position, through the customs and into Italy itself.

I saw the man, had lunch, and drove right back to France, taking the high road, the Grande Corniche.

Somewhere along it, high on the mountainside far above the sea and the shore, on a rather empty stretch of curving highway, I had a blowout. I changed the tire in the hot sun and drove on, wobblingly. The spare I'd used to replace it had a slow leak.

I managed to get to a gas station. It was closed; lunchtime in France. I waited. Finally the attendant came, but not the one who attended to tires. Another came, not the right one either. In fact, after a long time it developed that this gas station didn't do that kind of work. Not on this type of tire. Not when it had this particular kind of puncture.

A telephone call, a truck from Monte Carlo, a long wait for everything to be repaired, a large bill.

When at last I got back to Antibes, it was evening.

None of this would have made any difference except that I had agreed to meet Liliane on the beach that afternoon—"I want to talk about money," she had said, "so don't worry." I hadn't been worried; if *that* was all she wanted to see me about, I didn't mind. I was slowly running out of money, but money after all is replaceable, more can be earned. I didn't care if all she wanted to ask from me was money.

But I had missed the rendezvous, and now she might think that I was avoiding her because she mentioned money; she might think that in relation to her, money had some meaning for me. That was a bad possibility, and I didn't think Liliane would conclude that. But I wanted to make sure.

She wasn't at her hotel when I got back to Juan-les-Pins. I think it was because she had denounced the De la Croies the night before, that "corrupt family" whom she didn't wish to see again, I think it was because of that that I went there next to look for her.

Constance was alone in the refectory-like living room. She was sitting on a white couch sorting photographic slides; hundreds of them surrounded her singly and in little piles. Two black and gleaming cameras with complex attachments were at her feet.

"Hello! Come in! What a surprise! We were just talking about you. I'm sorry I can't get up, but if I move an entire year's record will just collapse in confusion."

"How are you this evening, Madame Constance? You say you were talking about me? How was that?"

"Well, Liliane was asking why—"

"She is here then?"

"Out in the boat," she went on offhandedly, "with Titou and Marc. They'll be back soon. In fact I believe they were going to look for you at Juan. I said I was sure you would come here." She looked briefly, directly at me. "You *were* delayed on the road, weren't you? I knew it was that. Liliane seemed so doubtful, so nervous. She is very attached to you, isn't she? A faint laugh was in her pleasure-filled voice. "I don't mean to pry, just ignore it, but I can't prevent myself from wondering if you shouldn't guard her more carefully, if your intentions, as one says, are serious. Nothing could possibly be less my affair. I'm sorry. Pay no attention to me at all."

God, I remembered, these people don't know I'm married to her.

"Of course Marc," she went on, studying one of her slides through a little viewer, "Marc is simply so attractive—I say it myself, brother or not—he is, isn't he? Yes; well, everyone in France knows it and so I've accepted it and talk about it now as though it were a car he owned, or a horse, for example. He is so attractive that he has naturally known a great many women and so of course he is not *serious* about Liliane at all. So you mustn't be jealous. You aren't, are you?"

"No."

"But then Liliane, lovely as she is, is not everyone's taste. I recognize that. Perhaps you don't—this picture will never be of any use to me." She tossed one of the slides into a wastebasket. "I can't concentrate on this any more, with such good company. Shall we go outside? If you would just move a few of these piles from my lap . . . yes, that one, yes. Now I will get these cameras out of the way. We shall go outside. Would you like a cognac, Scotch? They'll be back soon. Marc is bad about finding his way on the water at night. He won't risk staying out."

"Perhaps Titou is better."

"Titou? He—is no better. No."

Outside, the sea lisped among the rocks. The moon hung in place, and a protective Mediterranean silence settled around us. Constance offered me a cognac. As she passed between the back of my chair and the wall to reach the drinks, a narrow passage, her hands came unemphatically down on my shoulders, just for a moment, just a very short and cryptic message. "Isn't it peaceful here," she said, "calm? I come here for this, not for the sun or the sport or the society." She sighed a fragrant sigh. "Paris is so agitated. There are so many people, always some scandal to keep everyone disturbed." She shook her aura of wavy hair. "I shouldn't bother to keep up with all of that," laughing quickly to herself, "but Titou is a true gossip. He *must* tell me the latest excesses of all my friends."

"He even gossips about his own uncle."

"Yes!" a little startled, not quite knowing how to take that.

"There are plenty of scandals here on the Riviera for Titou to work on."

"It's true," she said, and I thought savagely about Marc and Liliane on the night sea, "but south of the Alps there are no rules. Nothing to be done about it. One must accept it. No?"

"Yes," I said, "Oh, yes, certainly, one must accept it."

"Would you . . . care to see the garden?" The garden was a prickly collection of cactus and other ugly tropical plants invisible now in the darkness.

"Yes, with pleasure." We started down the steps to it, I wondering what we were going to do in the dark; but that never passed the stage of wondering because there was noise in the living room and Titou came through the door to the terrace and said, "Don't run away just because we arrive. After all!"

"Hello!" Constance said with an air of pleased welcome, "There you are! I was beginning to worry about you! Hello Marc, Liliane! We were beginning to worry, weren't we?"

"Yes, we were beginning to worry."

"There was nothing to worry about," said Lili faintly. She was wearing close-fitted yellow pants, yellow blouse, and something straw on her head. I thought she looked irresponsible and beautiful.

"I had a puncture on the road," I said. "That's why I wasn't there this afternoon."

"It doesn't matter. I've made new plans, not expensive ones. It will save our—your money."

"Stop whispering," said Titou.

"I was just telling him about the cruise."

"What cruise?" I asked bluntly.

"I've chartered a boat," said Marc. "Yes, Constance, I finally settled on one; you'll like it, it sleeps eight, and crew. And so," to me, "Liliane has agreed to come with us for a few weeks."

"I see."

"My dear friend, that *was* a cold voice," Marc said with a conciliatory smile. "I am sorry. I did not mean to interfere with your friendship. But after all, you can't expect us to decline to take her when we have the chance. You can certainly see our point of view."

I turned away from him. "I don't want you to go," I said to her.

"*You* don't!" protested Titou.

Lili shook her head sadly at me. "Nicholas, you aren't supervising now."

"Yes," said Marc, "this country is free, as everyone insists. It's too free for its good, but never mind. My dear friend, you must admit that she is free to do what she wants without your permission."

"She's my wife," I said.

"Ah." This "ah" was familial; all three of them shared in it. They did not seem so much surprised as deeply interested; a deep new interest had just been created in both of us. Three pairs of clever, bright De la Croie eyes scanned us, almost appreciatively. Ah. Married. How interesting, they seemed to be thinking to themselves; these two aren't so simple as they look.

"Liliane," Marc nevertheless said in a reproachful tone, "you might, at least, my dear, have asked us to your wedding. Old friends like ourselves."

"We were married in America last year. We've been separated for nearly two months. I think you might have let me tell them in my own way and time."

"You didn't seem to be getting around to it ever."

"What *difference* does it make!" she said with abrupt intensity. "You don't want me! What *difference* does it make!"

"Why don't we—" Constance began.

"Why don't you stay away from me?" Lili drove on, "That's what you insist you want. Then why don't you!"

"I'm sorry I had to precipitate this," said Marc.

"I came because you were asking me for money, remember? I had a *blowout* and so I couldn't get here this afternoon and so I came this evening. In case you didn't have enough cash for dinner or anything. I knew where I could find you. With that corrupt family you were never going to see again."

"What!" cried Titou in amazement and delight. "What kind of family! Whose family!"

"I'll never touch a sou of yours for the rest of my life. I'll never have anyth—I'll never have—" and she started to cry.

Constance put her arm around her, Titou looked on piteously, and Marc said: "You are even more ridiculous as a husband. I presume you recognize that."

"Shut up, you Fascist."

Marc's eyes lighted up and an expression best described as "satisfied" flickered over his face. He had hoped to provoke me into some such wild outburst, and he'd succeeded. I had gone too far, instantly regretted it, couldn't do anything about it; he had tricked me. Why? For no particular reason, except that he knew I would regret it. He enjoyed making people do things they would regret.

I left then without another word. I had already said too many words.

"Nicky!" I heard as I got into my car. It was Titou. "You drive me into Juan? I want to go to the casino. This is everybody's lucky night, I notice. I'm going to try roulette." He bounced into the seat without bothering to open the door.

"Titou, I'm sorry about—"

"Listen, my pot, nothing you can say about us I haven't said myself. Better."

Off we shot down the drive. "How was the boat ride?" I asked.

"The boat ride. Oh, splendid, remarkable."

"Really?"

"Ah, yes. Unforgettable."

"So? Why?"

"Well, you see, it was the first time I ever took a boat ride without getting within a hundred meters of the water."

"What are you talking about?"

"I did not take a boat ride tonight."

"No?"

"No."

"It was Marc and Lili then."

"Yes. That displeases you?"

"But why did everyone lie to me, and say you had gone also?"

"Because of my uncle's reputation, I suppose. Everyone knows what he does with pretty girls in the boat after dark."

I turned a corner with a snap of the steering wheel and a cry from the tires.

"Careful! It's not worth killing us both. After all, she's only your wife. Look out! No, I'm sorry," his voice becoming slightly exasperated, "excuse me, eh. But frankly I meant it. She is not, for example, your mother."

"My mother."

"Your mother. In my own case you see, well . . . in my own case I am not able to get angry about anything. . . . Members of my family do. I am not able. Otherwise I would have been burned out inside, like—like an oil lamp. All my fuel would be gone."

With that hopeless subject before us we said nothing for a moment and then Titou, quickly, perhaps desperately regaining self-possession, said conversationally, "You would have been amused at the dinner conversation tonight."

"Is that so?" I said, conversationally too, two young men exchanging anecdotes.

"Yes. Lili and my mother and Marc and I were there. All of us —well, all of them because I was planning nothing complex—all three of them had their own little plots they wanted to hatch for the evening. What they wanted to do was of course the one thing they didn't talk about. Lili didn't say certain things about you and her arrangements for this evening and by that made it plain to my dear uncle that she was—"

"Free?" I hurriedly proposed.

"Available," he said at the same time. "My mother failed to mention any plans for *her* evening, which notified everybody that she was going to stay home and lay a bear trap for you. That suited all of them down to the ground. There remained only the problem of disposing of me. In this kind of conversation in our house you say only what will certainly not happen and so Lili said, 'Titou will come with us.' Everybody briefly said of course. And then I said I had to write a letter—in other words to humiliate them, making the weakest possible lie—I would never write a *letter*, on the *Riviera*, in the *evening*, and they knew it of course, but they all said: 'Oh, do you have to? Oh, too bad, what a pity! Well, we will have to manage the boat without you, somehow.' And then just as Uncle dear and Liliane were leaving, my mother said to them: 'You are going to look for Nicholas at Juan, aren't you? In case he comes here I will be able to tell him that, won't I?' Liliane immediately and energetically agreed to that, but my uncle looked slightly displeased. He doesn't like lies when they are designed to make people feel better. Still, he said nothing and so that motion of my mother's carried unanimously. Then they zoomed off to the Ile St. Marguerite, and my mother set her traps around the house—the chair where you would sit she moved close to the wall, for instance, so she would have to squeeze close to you. . . ."

Well, that was that, and even though I felt that I was bleeding to death hearing it, I drove on steadily to the casino.

"This has been such a lucky night for you," Titou said with a little grin of sympathy, "why don't you come in too?" So I did, and we played a half-baked form of roulette in the outer room reserved for the small spenders, and we both lost.

Then I drove him back to his house. Opposite the entrance to the driveway was a group of figures. They turned two big flashlights on us. One of them came forward; he was a policeman. He looked us and the car over very briefly, and said, "You live opposite, no?"

"I do, yes," said Titou. "What's going on?"

"Nothing important. Two Arabs made an attempt on another one, who lives there.' He gestured toward what seemed to be a doghouse collapsing against an old wall. "The Arab was out. We were in."

"You have good information these days, I see."

"By necessity. These Arabs! Always—" and he drew a blunt finger across his throat. Two shabby prisoners, black-haired and battered, stood staring at us, looking emaciated. The police officer saluted and we drove off.

"Very close to home this time," said Titou calmly. "Don't mention it to my mother. She is *très nerveuse*, you know."

"No, I never noticed that. She doesn't seem to be."

"Essentially she is. I think that is probably why she has all these, you know, why she has so many—"

"Yes. I see what you mean."

I stopped the car beside the house, and Titou sprang out, saying: "You won't come in? There may be a few unsprung traps still here and there. No? Well, then, good night. Dreams of gold."

At the end of the driveway I saw the police and the two Arabs still standing beside the wall. I got another salute as I drove by.

The baleful, distant hee-haw cry of a police wagon drifted along Cap d'Antibes, approaching rapidly; it was a sound both excited and depressed, hee-haw, hee-haw, coming from the other direction, the wagon careened by me on a curve, HEE-HAW, and dwindled swiftly into the distance again, toward the two skinny Arabs. In its wake the peculiar Mediterranean nighttime silence closed like the sea behind a racing ship.

||||||||||||||||||||

The next day I washed my car. They say women buy new hats to muffle tormenting emotions; perhaps that's what Lili did that morning.

It was a still morning on the Mediterranean. The sun burned with steady force everywhere in the empty blue sky. Very high in the blueness an airplane soundlessly led a single white line through space. Nothing moved that morning except the airplane halfway out of this world, and me, washing the car.

I had parked it at the end of an isolated alley, within three blank walls. Someone turned the corner and started down the alley toward me in the glare, a very dark young man, an Algerian; it was the one who had fixed my typewriter. He halted, standing there in his shabby clothes, and grinned at me. "Monsieur should not wash his car himself," he said in a soft voice. "That's for a laborer to do."

My hand tightened a little on the rag. There was no one else in sight except the pilot of that plane on the other side of the sound barrier. "It's all right," I said, laughing a little harshly, "I'm used to working."

He advanced a step and said, "Why exert yourself alone here in the hot sun? It's disagreeable for you. Me, I'm used to the heat and exertion. You allow me?" He came next to me and slowly began to take the rag out of my hand.

I felt the skin around my ears move as I brought a smile to my face and said, "I can do it myself."

"Ah!" an offhand gesture, "but I need the work!" The offhand gesture had gained him possession of the rag. "Otherwise I forget how. No matter." His dark eyes moved to my face. "You don't have to pay me."

The car was a convertible. The top was down. The key was in the ignition. Although he was not big he was muscular; in his blue canvas shorts and white undershirt the smooth muscles of his torso and legs worked easily as he rubbed the fender of the car.

"You're Algerian, aren't you?"

"Me?" He went on rubbing, and without turning his head, said, "No, Spanish."

"Do you still work with Sergio?"

"I work where I can. Anywhere. It's necessary to work, in order to live. Except perhaps," a little grin, "in America?"

"Perhaps." I could see already that he was doing a much better job than I had done in getting the car to shine.

"I will finish this little job—go over beside the wall, sit in the shade. I'm used to this sun. You see how brown I am, after all. You are too white for this sun."

He worked down to the wheels, the tires, then the floor inside— here was his chance to snap on the ignition and the motor and roar away down the alley. But something in the gentle, almost deferential way he went about cleaning it showed that this would not happen.

"Very beautiful buggy," he said, surveying it gleaming blue and silver in the sun, a neat and powerful little racer. "Will you take me for a short ride? I have never been in a car like this."

So we roared down the alley together, through the early-morning litter on the streets of Juan-les-Pins and out on the Cap d'Antibes road. He had asked me to drive to Golfe-Juan, a mile or two in the other direction, but I had a dim residual apprehension that there might still be a plot in this somewhere, confederates in some narrow street of Golfe-Juan, a garage with the door expectantly open, ready to slam after I had been forced in. Crime was like that on the Riviera; I was not being overimaginative. Everybody knew how the old Aga Khan had been stopped in broad daylight en route to the airport and his wife's jewels taken, the Aga contemptuously tossing money after the thieves—"Your tip!" Everyone knew about the movie producer whose wall safe was rifled during a delightful party. Everybody knew that on the Riviera life and crime were like that.

As we sped along by the sea, a figure coming erratically at us on a motor scooter revealed itself to be Titou. His face as he came closer expressed first pleasure, then interest, then amazement, then consternation, and then he was behind us. "The young De la Croie," remarked the Algerian.

"Do you know him?"

"In a way. I've seen him here and there. He is not serious."

We came up to the De la Croies' driveway and opposite it the shed. "He lives there," said the Algerian, pointing toward the villa.

"Do you know who lives there?" I asked, pointing toward the shed.

"There? That's a baker's helper—I—" He turned away. "I don't know."

"Someone attempted to kill the Algerian living there last night."

"Is that true?" he said vaguely. "These Arabs . . ."

"Listen. Tell the truth." Making this point at last made my foot heavier. We shot ahead across the end of Cap d'Antibes, past greenhouses and palms. "You are an Arab yourself."

After a moment he turned, and I glanced over at him. He had a bright, a playful, an almost beatific smile on his dark face. Then he said softly but definitely, "You are right!" watching me very carefully with sparkling eyes. "How did you know?"

"I knew. Why did you say you were Spanish?"

"Why not!" half angrily, half roguishly. "It's convenient. Anybody can say anything, no? What do you say you are?"

"I'm Russian."

"You see? Nobody tells the truth here." And he settled back satisfied in his seat as we came into the town of Antibes and on into Old Antibes, where in some crooked alley he had a room.

As I stopped the car to let him out, he suddenly decided to be forthright. Planting his fist firmly on his thigh he turned and said: "Listen. It's not worth it for me to say I'm Algerian to everybody. The French, they're a little afraid of us, I don't know why. And then, well, there are Algerians and there are other Algerians. We fight each other about this rebellion. We kill each other, that's the fact. We kill each other, I don't know why. It's strange. But there it is; it's not worth it to say I'm Algerian to everybody." He got out, and stood there hands on hips, suddenly exuberant. "But you know something? That's what I am! I'll see you later. You need more help, that can be seen. I'll pass by your apartment later." He threw up his hand in a kind of *torrero*'s salute. "Au revoir!" and he turned and walked, or waded, as though through sand, up a crooked little alley and out of sight.

I turned around in the narrow passage with difficulty, and drove back around Cap d'Antibes, past Titou's house, past the Hôtel du Cap and Mr. Warner's. In front of a rusticated restaurant ahead I saw Titou standing beside his motor scooter. I pulled up beside him.

"You're crazy, no?" he began at once. "Driving around with a terrorist in your car!"

"There's nothing terrifying about him so far."

"Of course not. That's their way. Gentle as silk until the knife to castrate you is firmly in place. Then—" His hand chopped down; he whistled. "Off! Did you hear about the raid they made on a French farm in Algeria? Afterward a seventeen-month-old baby was found there chopped in pieces," and he demonstrated the length of the baby and how it was chopped.

"Oh, for God's sake, Titou, do you believe that?"

"Yes!" he said firmly; then less firmly, "Why not?"

"If it's true, then some madman did it. Either army can have a madman in the ranks."

"Are you trying to say that the Army of the French Republic is no more civilized than a bunch of Arab bandits?"

"Yes."

So Titou and I stood between the palms and the wind-ruffled sea talking about war and death. That's the kind of season it was on the Riviera: water skiing and ideology in the daytime, the cha-cha-cha and assassinations at night.

"Liliane telephoned me this morning," he said. I sat unmoving with my hands on the wheel. "She discussed the weather. Then she said how good our dinner had been last night. She also asked me where I was planning to swim today. I had an urge to interrupt and say, 'Stop, Lili, and just tell me straight out whether you want some information about my Uncle Marc or about Nickie.' When she began telling me how nice the boat ride had been, how she had trailed her hand in the water—trailed her hand in the water! That boat goes forty miles an hour; when she got to that lovely-ride-in-the-moonlight story I finally did urge myself up to say, 'Lili, are you seeing Nickie or Uncle Marc today?' And she fell all into pretty confusion and said, Oh, well, she didn't know; after all it was very difficult; men were so sensitive, and what did I think? I told her I thought that if she really wanted to see you again she had better do so as quickly as possible because you were, what do you call it in English, the Wounded Party?"

"Yes," I didn't look up, "the Wounded Party."

"You were the Wounded Party and so it was her responsibility to make the move of reconciliation. After all, the only thing *you* got yesterday was a flat tire—well, aside from that little flirtation with my mother, I forgot that—while she and my uncle got . . . well, you know what they got."

I didn't say anything.

"So I think she will come around to find you and ask you to tea, for example. Make her pay! And now I've got to go. I'm having lunch in this restaurant with my mother and some hag friend of hers from Paris and some drug-addict official."

"Good appetite."

Laughter burst out of him. "Thank you a thousand times!" He laughed some more to himself. "Expect a visit from Lili. And keep away from that terrorist."

I thought to do the reverse would be a lot less risky.

||||||||||||||||||||||

Later I walked along the beach in the sun. Long rows of umbrellas so close together they touched sheltered long rows of mattresses. The umbrella shade cast a spell over the mattresses and white sand; under the umbrellas there was a glowing watery half-brightness shooting up from the surrounding blaze into this shade, creating a half-tone shimmer, an indistinct filmy radiance, a lax gleaming outline to the people lying there. From one of the mattresses Jimmy Smoot rose up like a water buffalo and said nasally: "Nick! It's you. Come here, I've got so much to tell you."

"Hello, Jimmy. Do you? What is it?" Jimmy always had had much to tell me and everybody else because he recounted every purchase down to toothpaste and a comb, everywhere he had been, including the bank to change a traveler's check, what he'd had for dinner and breakfast, how the weather struck him, what time it was. But today was different; he really had something to tell. Sergio had taken him in hand.

So, uncharacteristically, he hesitated, glanced doubtfully at me, smiled an abashed, almost sweet smile, and finally in his Philadelphia voice said, "Nick, I'm engaged."

I looked at him practically writhing there on the mattress and all I could find to say was, "Go on."

No one had ever had to say that to Jimmy before. He looked very startled and then puzzled and then said, "I don't know where to begin."

"Begin with Sergio."

"How funny. That was quite a guess, Nick, because as a matter of fact, you're right! It *does* begin with Sergio. You remember when you introduced me to him the other day?"

After a brief pause I said, "Yes."

"We went for a drive in the Porsche, and we got along awfully well right from the start. We were *sympathique,* that's the way he put it. *Sympathique.* It doesn't mean sympathetic. It means when you understand someone instinctively right from the start. It happens between two people who are basically similar. It's happened to me before, but I never knew there was a word for it. *Sympathique.* Say it."

"*Sympathique.*"

"Sergio and I are very *sympathique,* and that's what makes him think of Josée. She used to be his fiancée but they had to break it off because—he was very frank about it, Nick—he and Josée were from different classes. I knew they had different classes in England but I didn't know they still had them in France. Didn't the Revolution remove all that? Apparently not, because that was why they couldn't get married. Josée's class was quite a few higher and they knew they couldn't make a go of it. They're very practical about things like that here, aren't they?"

"Yes." I wish, I added in the inner soliloquy I'd been carrying on since seeing Lili in that little straw hat come back from the boat ride with Marc, I wish I were.

"Sergio and Josée couldn't make a go of it, so now he's engaged to another girl and the same day you introduced me to him *he* introduced me to Josée. She's here. She lives in Paris, in the Sixteenth Arrondissement, which is like Park Avenue in New York, but she's here for a vacation now, and Nick, she's so chic. I mean real continental chic, hair all on one side; it's red, dyed, but the right way. You look at her and you just think of Class. Everything is the latest style. Silver fingernail polish. She knows how to dress." Here something gripped him, he flushed, and looked down, his mouth in an uncontrollable grin, and he added, "and undress."

"You made love to her that first night?"

"*No!* Who do you think I'm marrying, a call girl? I mean she knows how to wear a bathing suit, resort clothes, halters. You know. Something different all the time. I think she must be loaded with money. She's such wonderful company, Nick. We have every meal together at the Victory. Yes, Sergio has the chef make special dishes for us. Bouillabaisse and *ratatouille* and special native things like that." Jimmy laughed in his level, faintly unreal way, as though rehearsing for a real laugh later on. "Nick, she's so entertaining, the best company you ever saw. Her English isn't very good. In fact she doesn't speak it. But Sergio's such a good translator. There's one thing, though—did you ever notice how much longer it takes to say something in French than it does in English? The two of them sit there talking back and forth, back and forth, and finally I'll say, 'What did she say?' and Sergio translates: 'She's heard so much about America.' That's all! It's amazing how long it takes to say that in French. Of course, they're so much more elaborate in everything they do. I suppose they speak the same way. I'm talking to you like an American. I think of you as American. What are you, anyway?"

"I'm American."

"Anyway, the point is, I'm *happy!* Just think, me, with a French wife! Madame Jameson Smoot, of Ardmore, Pennsylvania." He gave me that guilty-ecstatic smile of his. It was a winning smile, because it made this bald thirty-five-year-old man look like a delighted boy, happy at the center of his own wonderful world, a boy's world, of Scout Honor and roller-coaster rides and corn silk. "I have something to show you." He rummaged among the equipment he always brought to the beach with him—camera, sun-tan lotion, portable radio, a flask of mineral water, green eyeshade, and found a small box. It contained some engraved cards. "I had these made; I couldn't resist seeing how it would look." The cards read:

M. et Mme. Jameson Smoot
Les Pins
Ardmore, Pennsylvanie

"What are Les Pins?"

"That's what we'll call our house. We're going to live in a house the family owns out there in the country. It's called Happynest right now. I never really liked that name. Les Pins has, you know, style. With Josée there it'll be appropriate, Nick. After all, our romance started right here, in Juan-les-Pins. I told her about changing the name of the house last night, and she was thrilled after I explained how significant it was, since our romance started here. She was fascinated when I described the house to her too. She's so *enthusiastic*, Nick! You never met anyone so gay, laughing all the time. We communicate by laughing. When you're *sympathique* with a person you don't need language, do you? We communicate—our way of talking, Nick—I call it the language of laughter. That's a poetic way of putting it, isn't it? Well," that smile beginning again, "I've told you everything about it. Aren't you going to congratulate me?" The question was not coy and not playful. At bottom, it was anxious. He'd told me everything. How did I evaluate it? *Was* I going to congratulate him?

"Jimmy, congratulations and all the best wishes. I hope everything works out wonderfully, and of course I want to meet Josée as soon as possible. Still, you're not going to get married right away, are you?"

"She's in quite a hurry!"

"Not right away. You have to tell your family, for one thing."

"That's true."

"Wait a few weeks, at least. You're going to, aren't you?"

"Oh, of course. I don't know how my family will take it," he said, gazing vacantly up at the umbrella. "I had a letter from Dad today."

That was always bad news. But I couldn't help being glad about all these disasters that had been visited on Jimmy—a trumped-up engagement, a letter from his father—because they momentarily made me feel a little bit better about myself. It was the usual ignoble human response; I couldn't help it.

Jimmy's Dad. As the son gazed up at the underside of the bright umbrella, I recalled that the father was a formidable supplier of misery for Jimmy. Misery and money. Mr. Smoot was an almost grotesquely vigorous eighty-four. He owned and remorselessly operated a string of clothing stores, a television station, a baseball team, four hotels, two nonpicturesque but very prosperous ranches, and several restless oil wells. From everything Jimmy had told me about his home life, and that was a lot, I gathered that Mr. Smoot couldn't really stand Jimmy. The old man had experienced the one shadow over his perfect health—a heart attack—the Thursday he came home for lunch and found Jimmy having breakfast in a Chinese dressing gown. He had already tried setting Jimmy up as a weekly newspaper publisher, a farmer, a designer of men's resort shirts, an art-gallery operator, and a florist. Jimmy was now on his newest set-up, arranged immediately after the heart attack. This new career was traveling. Once again the specter of failure hovered: he had spent a few days in London, a few days in Paris, and now here he was lolling on the same mattress on the same beach at Juan-les-Pins hour after hour, week after week. He could not publish or grow things or design or sell pictures or flowers, and now it was becoming clear that he could not travel either. He could only stay. Looking at him now, I remembered that some sage, Freud perhaps, had said that the crucial moment in a male's life occurs when his father dies. And perhaps it was that event that Jimmy was numbly and dumbly waiting for.

I left him there doing it and went to look for Sergio.

I had always had good sense. People always talked their problems over with me because of this good sense of mine. "You're so controlled," they said, "so balanced." They said this before I met Liliane and married her three weeks later, fell in love with the uncontainable excitement I saw in her and married her. They said it through the year of gathering disaster that followed, because I continued to have so much good sense about their problems. And now they are beginning to say it again. Good sense. Except when I was completely out of my senses, all of them were good.

Now I would have to see if I couldn't do something about this "engagement." Other people's problems, other people's problems! Thank God, I said to myself as I waded through the sand, for other people's problems. It was all right for Sergio to traffic in black-market francs if he wanted to, to smuggle back and forth into Italy, to sell marijuana cigarettes to the Arabs and Parisians, but it was not all right for him to marry this overage playgirl to that defenseless American. She wasn't even divorced from her first husband. There was a child. Jimmy obviously hadn't heard about either of those. Sergio would probably be even more pleased if he could have Jimmy marry bigamously: he would see possibilities for even greater profit in that.

I liked Sergio, he was so true to himself. He was also as characteristic of the Riviera as olive oil. He and the other Provençals could understand every vice and every failing in man except Jimmy's: not being himself. Bravado, putting up a front, yes; but deep distrust of himself, no. If Jimmy gave his trusting, nervous, boy's heart to someone and then found he had married into a confidence game, it would be the end of Jimmy.

Mireille came along the beach toward me. Her skin was tobacco brown and she wore a pale yellow bikini. Her lipstick was white. She carried her toy poodle.

"Have you seen Sergio?"

"No," she said. "Or, yes. Perhaps. I think so, somewhere."

"I'm looking for him. Try to think. I have something important to see him about."

"Do you?" she said vaguely, stroking the dog's muzzle. "Look out for Sergio and his affairs, eh? You involve yourself with him and you'll finish in manacles. A little contraband is all right, if he wants, but Sergio goes too far! Look out for him," and she trailed off, stroking the dog.

It's hot, I thought to myself, really hot.

Max was stamping up and down on his section of the beach. He was, in the most masculine way, a beautiful young man. His strong and orderly face, nose, jaw, mouth, forehead, seemed more than any man's face I had seen to be radiant, to send forth almost visible rays, yellow ones, matching the hair sweeping back from this strong and orderly face. Someone who looked like him must have inspired the first concept of godlike qualities in men.

"Hi, you clown," he said to me, "and who are we going to bounce tonight? I kicked out that broad from Antibes. We've got to find some other dupes, no?"

"Max, I'm looking for Sergio. It's important." And I explained about Jimmy and the engagement. Max followed it with bright, concentrating eyes.

"Not stupid, Sergio," he commented. "Of course, unless Sergio has some special hold on her this girl is never going to let him have another sou once she's in America. There's that disadvantage to his plan." And as I was leaving, his last remark was, "I'd like to meet your friend from Philadelphia. Not pederast, is he? No. Well, all the same, I'd like to meet him. So long, old pal."

I caught sight of Sergio coming along amid the throng of legs, stomachs, arms, and hair that made up the movement of the Juan-les-Pins promenade. In his white waiter's jacket and black pants he walked with a snap, an assertive Franco-Italian strut.

"Sergio, what do you think you're doing—"

"Hello, my old friend, aren't there more and more people here every day? It's fine! The Big Season has really begun!"

"My friend Jimmy Smoot has just told me—"

"He's coming to lunch at the Victory. Why don't you come too? Do you know that he has had *every meal* there since you were kind enough to introduce me to him? I find that very friendly."

"But was it friendly of you to involve him with that Parisienne?"

"It was nothing." He kept walking rapidly along. "I wanted to do something for both of them, my old friend and my new. It was no effort."

"If you wanted to start a little affair that's one thing, but this marriage business!"

"I know. It took me completely by surprise too. Who would have thought?"

"You would have thought, if I know you."

"No, no, I can't take any credit."

"Credit! For inveigling him—"

"Her charm did it. And his charm too, naturally."

"She's *married!*"

"Don't worry. They have already started about the divorce. That won't ruin their happiness."

"With a child!"

58

"That is what she is going to show Monsieur Jimmy, for a grand surprise. Her mother will bring it down from Paris. He loves children. I've already noticed. It's unheard of, the luck of this couple!"

"Are you pretending that this is serious!"

"Ah, one must dare in life, to win the great prizes. Here we are. Come in. Sit at the bar until the happy ones arrive," and marching smartly, he led me into the Victory.

After a while Jimmy and Josée arrived. She was a rather tall girl. "Enchanted, Monsieur," she murmured. Her fingernails were silver and her hair was a nonflaming red, I'd expected that much; but I hadn't expected a certain anxious look on her face. She looked pretty and disillusioned and nervous. Her beach shirt had blue and white diamond-shaped checks, and her slacks were black.

"You're just in time for lunch with us," Jimmy said in his matinee voice; "we always sit over there," pointing to a table just inside the frontless restaurant. "Come on. You haven't eaten, have you? The food is good here, Nick, it's *parfait*. No, Josée? Ha-ha." Laughing with care he led us to the table. "You can translate, all right, Nick? Sergio has to work for a while, I guess. *Bon jour, Sergio! Comment ça va? Bien? Bien. Moi aussi, ça va très. . . .*

Sergio said: "*Toi aussi? Ah c'est bon, ça. Il faut. Si ça ne va pas quand on est fiancé, ça n'ira jamais, non?*"

"Ha-ha. Josée is learning English too."

Josée was studying Jimmy every time he looked away from her. It might be thought of as love, the feeling expressed in this steady look of surmise, or it might be amazement or disbelief. But what it looked most like was simple wonder. What was this man who laughed often? He wanted to marry her. She couldn't grasp any single thing about him. Her face smiled steadily when he looked at her, and when he didn't this simple bafflement came over it. Jimmy and I talked while we ate, and with the dessert I began talking to her about the weather.

"Wonderful," I said.

"Unbelievable."

"I don't remember a more beautiful summer."

"Neither do I."

"No."

"I really don't."

"I believe you."

"Nick," said Jimmy, "you're just as bad as Sergio. You keep talking to her and never translate anything. What have you been saying?"

"We said it was a beautiful day."

"You did! All those words—oh, you're kidding me." He threw back his head, and laughed. "No, Nick, you've got to tell me: what were you really saying?"

"I was going to ask her if she loved you."

The half-artificial glee drifted out of his face, leaving it first empty and then full of uneasiness. "Go on," he finally said huskily, "ask her."

"Jimmy, that was a joke. The weather was serious."

She was tugging at my shirt. "What did you say to him? What is he asking? He looks angry."

"No, no. He's not at all angry."

"Go ahead and ask her," he said more firmly.

"If you could talk to each other you could ask her yourself. That's the only normal way. I can't ask her."

"I'm sure he's getting angry. You are saying unfriendly things about me, Monsieur?"

"I assure you, Mademoiselle, I am not. We were discussing language."

" 'Long' what?" Jimmy cut in insistently. "I speak *some* French, you know. You said we were discussing 'long' something."

"Languages, Jimmy, languages. *Langues.*"

"Oh."

"You can't pretend that he isn't angry *now.*"

"Not at you. At me, perhaps."

"He is defending me. I understand. He will not permit his fiancée to be criticized in his presence. That is kind. Unlike you, Monsieur, with your bad disposition."

60

"What did she say, Nick?" and now Jimmy did seem on the verge of getting angry, "She says I have a dirty mind? I caught that last part."

" 'Bad disposition,' not 'dirty mind.' And she was talking about mine, not yours."

Then Josée slid her silver-nailed hand across the pink tablecloth into his. "Oh," he said, taking it, the big smile breaking, "Oh. I got it all wrong. What does she want to say now, Nick?"

I thought of getting up and walking away, but instead I turned to Josée with a sigh and said, "What do you wish to say to him now?"

She looked quickly from side to side, blinking, and then Jimmy, gazing directly at her, opened his mouth and with his nostrils dilated he began to laugh. Josée looked at him in alarm. "Laughter, Nick," he said, "the best thing in the world. We have our language of laughter. Who needs words? She understands."

The tension left her eyes and she slowly began to smile. Her hand tightened in his and the two of them looked straight into each other's faces, laughing hard.

Some of the other diners stopped eating to stare frankly at them; Sergio paused en route to the kitchen to weigh the situation, and they kept laughing. Neither wanted to be the first to stop. Feeling awkward I turned and looked out at the street. A gray-green truck, carrying laundry perhaps, was coming along the beach-side street, deserted now for the noontime meal. It came abreast of the restaurant, going slowly. People in the restaurant found their attention being pulled from the two people strangely laughing in each other's faces to the gray-green truck—a soldier was at the wheel—going by. The back half of the truck was covered with a tarpaulin, so that it was past the restaurant before we saw that leaning against the tailgate there were soldiers, fully uniformed for combat, with what looked like small machine guns whose muzzles were turned toward the rear opening of the truck.

Jimmy, seeing them, laughed once or twice more with particular hollowness and then stopped. Then Josée stopped. The soldiers were youthful and looked relaxed. Twenty-year-olds in big helmets holding machine guns. I suddenly realized that there were two parts of my body particularly vulnerable to bullets: my head and my stomach. The truck continued to make its way slowly along the street, creating a fog of silence behind it. It was possible to imagine bullets snapping around the street, ricocheting between the Blue Club and the Victory.

"What was that?" Jimmy demanded across the table. "Who were they? Is there some kind of trouble around here? What's going on in this country, anyway? Here's today's paper—I bought it to see what the movies were in Cannes. Look at those headlines! Black! What's going on around here anyway?"

He handed me the paper. The front page was crowded with headlines:

CRIMINAL OUTRAGE IN ALGIERS
19 Wounded

THREE PEOPLE KILLED AND TWO WOUNDED IN PARIS BY ALGERIANS FIRING FROM A MOVING CAR

Three French Nobel Prize Winners, Roger Martin Du Gard, François Mauriac and Albert Camus, Have Been Invited To Form a Committee Charged To Investigate the Claimed Atrocities in Algeria

A NORTH AFRICAN FOUND WITH A KNIFE IN HIS BACK IN AN UNDERPASS AT CANNES

I translated no more for Jimmy; he was looking and listening wordlessly. Then he cried: "Why didn't you say anything about this! You could have said something about it. *You know* I can't read French. All you ever talk to me about is clothes and Philadelphia. You could have warned me what was happening in this country. I'm a stranger here. Where's Sergio? I want the check. Let me pay for this, Nick. I invited you and I'm paying. Josée, are you ready to go?

Josée can't leave this country for months. I know what all the paper-work is like. Months! Sergio, *viens ici un moment. L'addition,* Sergio. Did you see those soldiers and guns? *I* never knew there was a war going on here."

"Not a war, no war. The war is over there," waving at the Mediterranean, "the other edge of the sea, in North Africa. Far, far away. Here we have peace, as always. Have a cognac. Yes, please. I pay." Jimmy was already on his feet. "You will not accept a cognac from me?"

He sat slowly down again. "Why do I have to be the one to think things through around here? Everybody else is so—I don't know—*bland.* What's the matter with you?" he said to me. "Aren't *you* worried?"

Nobody had asked me that until now, and I hadn't asked my-self. "I—I have to admit things are disorderly," I said, and then added, "They tried to kill a man across the street from the De la Croies last night."

Jimmy's eyes snapped at me. "You wouldn't have told me," he said bitterly, "unless we'd seen those soldiers. You never would have warned me!"

"I didn't think it had anything to do with you," I said, "or me either."

"Well, what do you think now?"

"Now?" Sergio came and put down three glasses of cognac. "Now I'm beginning to think it does."

We picked up our glasses. Josée looked from one to the other. "Here's to peace," said Jimmy grimly.

"To Josée," I said at the same time.

"To *Josée!*" he exclaimed as though he'd sat on a tack, swinging around with a hasty grin. She blinked several times and then quickly emptied her glass, set it back on the table, sighed, and looked vacantly, a little bleakly too, out to sea. She could only have had a sketchy idea of what Jimmy had said, but something in it had touched her seam of disillusionment. This chance, too, with a man looked bad. Something was the matter with him. He was all up in the air just then. Men were supposed to be firmly planted on the ground, so women could moor themselves to them. This one saw a few boys in uniform, and up he went! Something was the matter. It was beginning to look as though this affair was going to be like the others. Nowhere to moor.

||||||||||||||||||||

That afternoon I took a nap in my apartment. Because of the heat, the wine and cognac at lunch and general exhaustion, I fell into the drugged sleep that comes from sleeping at an unaccustomed time of day.

The door buzzer electrocuted my dream. I nearly fell getting out of bed, and made my way cloudily to the door, got it open with difficulty, and perceived Lili. "May I come in?" she asked. She looked at me, noticed the rumpled bed through the door, and seemed to realize that I was half-drugged with unnatural sleep.

An altered look, of concentrated, blank energy, came into her eyes. She slid her arms under mine, held my mouth against hers, leaned toward the bedroom door, went at my shirt buttons, my belt. I saw her intent eyes, her eyebrows curving over them; I saw her mouth. It was Liliane. I couldn't remember what I had to forgive her for. Half undressed, we two slowly and clumsily rocked together into the bedroom. She could not seem to bear to break contact with my body at any point, and when we had struggled out of all our clothes, there was no need to, at last.

||||||||||||||||||||

At the time of evening when my apartment began to sail on the tops of the pines, black under the deep night-blue sky, I woke up again. Someone was in the kitchen. Liliane. I slowly remembered, stage by stage, the afternoon, the buzzer, the drug of sleep, Liliane's eyes, intent, fixed, possessed. This afternoon I had opened the door and Liliane walked in, and the moment she entered the atmosphere of my laxness, my sleep, she was transformed into somebody else. People do turn into somebody else sometimes. You don't have to be hit over the head for it to happen. I saw now that this was what took possession of Liliane with other men. This was the first time it had happened to her with me. Now, for whatever good it would ever do me, I knew.

It is very hard when the most intense pleasure of your life has also been the most severe shock.

I went into the kitchen. She was wearing something softly pink, standing in the blue-gray dusk beside the stove, the little jets of flame vaguely lighting a glint of something on her finger, a tiny sparkle at her throat, and sending faint wavering lights across her intent face. She turned from the stove and said: "I hate to turn on the light. I like it just the way it is. Don't you?" Glowing in the dark, with these few gleams about her picked out by the tiny flames, she suddenly reminded me of a southern bird I had once seen caught in a cage and seeming content to be caught, assumed tame and all the old instincts quenched, a house pet now; in any case no one knew about the old rages, no one could tell; and all the while its wild markings glowed treacherously on, acclaiming a mad life in the sky and in the jungle treetops, that kind of past, that kind of future.

Liliane said: "I'm making a little supper for us. Everything is ready but I didn't want to start cooking until you woke."

She went to the window, like some pink sprite slipping through the blueness, and for a moment I half thought she would step across the sill and glide and fade deeper into the darkening blue sky, glide away, escape, and shine with her true brightness when the moon rose again.

"I have some salami, and some lettuce, and there are a couple of eggs. Do you want wine or just mineral water?" Something clattered to the floor. "I can't find the frying pan. Damn."

I reached for the light switch. Yes. Damn. Yes.

I turned on the light. It was a typical French bulb, raw, naked, yellow. It brought up the brown-and-white kitchen, the blue-and-white stove, the yellow dishes, and Liliane standing in the middle in an expensive resort outfit.

"The frying pan's under the sink," I said.

She turned toward the miniature refrigerator. "Where?" she said vaguely.

"Under the sink."

She had the refrigerator door open, and bending down she shifted among the bottles of water, plates of butter, bowls of cold vegetables. "Would you get it for me?"

I got it and put it down next to the sink.

"Will what I mentioned be enough," she said, "or do you want a main course?"

"That'll be enough, I guess."

"You aren't sure."

"I guess it will. There's some cheese."

"You mean to mix with the eggs? A cheese omelet?"

"I was thinking of it for dessert, but a cheese omelet—"

"Oh, yes, as dessert. That's much better. What kind of cheese is it?"

"It's there, on top of the refrigerator," I said, pointing.

"I don't see it."

"It should be there."

"It must be here somewhere. Cheese, cheese."

"I don't really want cheese anyway, if it isn't there."

"You don't? What'll we have for dessert, then? Would you like dessert?"

"I guess not; I don't care."

"I am trying to make a good meal, Nick—"

"Of course, I know. What you have there is fine, Lili."

"I'll start the omelet." She stood in front of the stove, its little jets overwhelmed now by the bulb. "The frying pan is—?"

"Right there, beside you."

She looked to the wrong side.

"The sink. Next to the sink."

66

She started to reach for it and her tan arm stopped midway. After another second her head turned toward me. "You don't want to eat, do you?"

"No." I was very hungry. "Yes, I'd just as soon, if you want to fix it."

"Do you want me to fix it?"

"If you'd like to, why—"

She put her hands on the stove and, glaring at the wall, said, "Do you want me to fix it?"

"Of course I do. Why not?"

"Why not!"

"I mean, you're here and—"

"I barged in, you mean, so you might as well let me."

"Come on, Lili. The thing's half ready." I went over to the sink, to wash my hands or do something else. "You're nervous tonight."

"My eye is going to swell up. I can feel it. I know it's going to start again. First you ask me . . ."

"Hum?"

"First you want to eat, then . . ." She took the frying pan. "I can't make an omelet in this."

"Why not?"

"This is for—God knows. Where is your real frying pan?"

"This is it. This is the only frying pan there is."

"It's going to be a miserable omelet. Who ever heard of a kitchen with just that for a frying pan." She fumed over the stove for a minute. "Here, I can't use this. I'll do something else. This is useless. Put it back." She handed me the frying pan.

I didn't like the way she spoke or the way she handed it to me. I took it, and everything about her then froze in my mind into unforgivability; in one motion I hurled the frying pan across the kitchen and through the only partly open window, a good throw, and it went swaying on the air far into the blue-black evening, tilting and swaying among the palms and pines. Only after some time was there a small remote clatter somewhere.

"Oh, you're absolutely mad! You're crazy! If you hit someone—"

"I didn't hit you with it, did I? Be glad and just worry about yourself!"

"You're crazy and you're insulting! I asked you to put something—"

"Who asked you anything? Who asked you here? Who asked you into my—"

"Bed?" she said in a quiet way, standing still.

"Apartment," I said, over this.

She looked me directly in the eye, face closed, and said, nodding slightly, "You are vicious, aren't you?"

"I'm vicious! That's really rich. I'm vicious! I go away for a day and you're making love to that French Fascist."

"You and his sister—No! I won't discuss any of this. I've got to get out of here and I've got to get out now."

"Through the window or the door?"

"*I've got to get out of here!*" She was going to be hysterical, clutching the side of the stove.

"Stop! Stop screaming. Get out," I said. "I'll show you how. Get out."

The buzzer sounded. Lili, mumbling, "Oh, good God, I've got to get out of here!" made her way quickly into the bedroom and closed the door. The buzzer sounded again. The people next door were coming to complain about the noise. Or had I really hit someone with the pan? Nothing to do but face it.

I opened the door. Jeannot the Algerian, almost dancing with amusement, stood there holding out the frying pan. "You missed her," he said, looking at me with new interest and delight. "I saw it fall out of your window." He was very pleased. There was a woman with me; we yelled at each other and threw things. What a fine household to work in! He came through the doorway, a small round cap on the back of his shiny black hair, and carrying a little round canvas sack with drawstrings.

"How do you know I threw it?" I said, taking the pan.

"I told you. I saw it come through your window."

"Maybe she threw it."

"She? The woman? It's the men who throw things."

"You really are an Arab."

"Did she?"

"No, I threw it," I said over my shoulder, going into the kitchen with the pan.

"Ah, the kitchen!" His brightened eyes swept over the preparations for the meal. He put down the little sack, an Arab accessory that lost any feminine associations in his hand, and moved purposefully to the stove, "I'm going to recommence—"

"Listen, Jeannot. Thank you for returning the pan. But I don't need a servant, couldn't pay for a servant, and above all not now. You have hit a bad moment, as you see." But he didn't seem to see at all; there was not a fleck of embarrassment; he thought his arrival couldn't have been more opportune: a family fight, the perfect entrée for a servant, we needed him. "—But thank you for the pan. Let's have a drink together soon."

"She's crying, undoubtedly," he said in a low voice, with frowning eyes and smiling mouth, tilting his head toward the bedroom. "Go," he said, falling into the intimate French singular, "go and become friends again. It's better, no? I'm going to prepare you a little meal, to help."

"But I told you I can't have a servant."

"Afterward I am going to leave. But this is a present, to give me pleasure. All right?"

There was an impatient noise from the bedroom. "Wait a minute," I said, and went to the door and stepped inside. Liliane was sitting on the bed with her hands in her lap. "Who is it?" she asked in a flat voice. "Close the door." And then her voice began to waver. "Please, get rid of whoever it is. Will you do that for me?"

"Yes, of course. It's an Arab I know."

"Can you ask him to come back later?"

The Arab suddenly became useful. "I can't do that. You see, he works here now. He's fixing dinner. That's why I didn't think you should do it. I knew he was coming."

She looked at me for the first time and said, "Well why didn't you say so?" She went on pondering me. "You might at least have said so." She stood up. "All this fuss . . . Is he a good cook?"

"He's—why, yes, yes, he certainly is. You'll see. You will— Will you stay and have something to eat? Why not? And then we can—"

"All right, yes, all right. Later we can talk about—"

"Yes, later on we can."

We went together out of the bedroom and into the kitchen. She greeted Jeannot with an overwhelming graciousness born of gratitude, and he greeted her with twinkling formality. The two of them quickly opened a detailed discussion of sauces and herbs and omelets and finally, tentatively and then uproariously, of frying pans.

Dinner, amid a steady swift current of French between the two of them, was gradually served. The salami had little black burning points in it, small explosions of seasoning; the salad—just lettuce— was given a dressing that made it arch, as though in transit to some higher level of taste, reaching; the omelet contained certain dark intimations. Bread, a large golden-ridged twist of French bread, went with everything; here it still was the staff of life. We drank *rosé* wine from a chilly bottle shaped like a vase for flowers.

"Nick didn't tell me you worked here," she said to Jeannot. And she said, "How long have you lived in France?" and, "Do you miss North Africa?" and, "Have you a family there?" and, "Have you suffered from this detestable war?" and, "You must show me how to make such an omelet. Let's see, you put . . ." and, "Will you be able to tolerate working for Monsieur Bodine? He's Russian, after all. Nicholas Petrovich Bodine. Yes, incredible, I agree. All right, half-Russian, by descent. Slavic at heart, all the same. Or perhaps Mongolian . . . look at those eyes. You notice how they go up a little at the ends? That cold blue color? Those prominent cheekbones? Coarse mouth? You see all that, Monsieur Jeannot? Don't expect a free-spending American. They let him into their country, but that's all. The half that isn't Slavic is Parisian French. You understand, pinchpenny. Cynical. There you have Nicholas Petrovich

Bodine: an emotional Slav, either in ecstasy or in despair, combined with a calculating Parisian shopkeeper." Lili had been drinking a lot of the *rosé*. Jeannot, taking all this for the best of good clean fun, couldn't see to eat for laughing.

"But I thought," he managed to choke out, "everybody here on the Riviera thinks that all the Old Russians are princes and dukes. True, no?"

"All except Nicholas Petrovich Bodine. I'm sorry; he is not even an Admiral. Do you know what he is? He's middle class. Did you ever hear of anything like it in your life? Middle class. A *middle-class* White Russian. *Of course*, all the others are Grand Dukes. But not him. I don't know if you're familiar with the bourgeoisie in Old Russia. Well, let me familiarize you, a little. They were the most foolish, the silliest, the most ineffectual class in the history of any country anywhere. No, no, it's true, true. Here, a little more bread, to clean up the rest of that omelet. There. Yes," she went on after gulping some more *rosé*, and glancing gleefully and yet confusedly at me, "it's true, true, isn't it, darling? It was you who told me so."

"Yes, I told you so."

"And so, my dear Monsieur Jeannot, it will help you to understand your dear employer if you know about this Old Russian bourgeoisie. You see, it's this that happened. They waited for three centuries, under an awful tyranny by the tsar and the aristocrats, they waited all that time to develop enough and be strong enough to have *their* turn to run the country. Every other middle class in Europe succeeded in doing that. But not them! After waiting for three centuries the revolution finally came in 1917 and the middle class finally got the power, and do you know how long they kept it?" Jeannot shook his dark head. "Six months! After waiting three centuries! Isn't that the most unheard-of thing in the world! No, no, Monsieur Bodine doesn't mind our discussion. It was he who told me all this. It's all right, don't be disturbed. I told you, this will help you understand him . . . his moods . . . his odd moods . . . gaiety . . . unhappiness for nothing . . . so many things. Frying pans! You'll see, it's very important to understand all that. He, his whole family, all of them, they're like bombs that never went off. You'll see."

"Me too," said Jeannot stoutly, "I'm a bomb. But me, I go off!"

"Yes, yes," she said, suddenly weary, "yes, I'm sure you do. Did someone say something about coffee? Nick? Nicholas? Would it be all right," switching to English, "if I had a little coffee? May I?" And then, looking depressed, she added, "I'm sorry. I'm terribly sorry. I can't help myself today." She spoke so softly I could hardly hear her words, "You were right to get away from me. You were right."

"I'll get the coffee," I said. Liliane never drank much. But she had worked herself up to this gaiety deliberately; it was an odd, final gaiety, it seemed to me, and that's why I didn't join it or block it. I watched it in surmise; it was the gaiety of a ship's sailing, or of a wake.

I walked to her hotel with her, through the palm-planted black streets, past sculptured ghostly house fronts, in the wide, waiting silence of the Mediterranean nighttime; we walked toward the gathering pulsations of the center of town, the milky lights, and on through the center to the silent, monumental hotel where she stayed.

Liliane had become talkative again, chattering on steadily in her breakable voice: "There's a piano in this hotel, so now I can practice again, thank God. It's in the ballroom and nobody else ever gets up before noon, so I can use it all morning without anyone bothering me. I suppose I bother *them*, but no one has complained so far. I'm still working on the Debussy, and I think I'm getting closer to it. I really think I am. Years of learning to play with absolute clarity, and now I have to learn to blur! Well, I suppose that happens not only in music; I suppose that happens in life too . . . perhaps if I could blur a little—Did you ever smell anything like these trees! I want to give you the key to your apartment—"

"You have a key to my apartment?"

"Our apartment. In Paris."

"Oh."

72

"I haven't it with me. I'll get it to you tomorrow."

"I don't need it. I have my key."

"Of course, but . . ."

"I don't expect to go back there for a while. Keep it; you might want to use the apartment if you happen to go back to Paris this summer."

"I'll get it to you tomorrow."

"I—I'm sorry about that frying pan."

"A real Russian."

"I lost my temper."

"Yes, yes, well I know what it is," she said quietly, "losing control of yourself."

"I am sorry. I'm feeling a lot better, and in a few more weeks I'll be all right."

"I know you will. I'm not going to—hinder that any more."

"You don't exactly hinder anything, Liliane."

"Why did you say that? It's not the truth."

"I said it because I wanted to—I wanted it to be true. Because of the way these trees smell, these rose trees or whatever they are."

"Yes, I see."

We reached the door of the hotel. There was no one anywhere. There were the white gravel under our feet, the superb doorway in front of us, and beyond it the great white vaulting empty lobby. "Goodbye, Nick," she said.

"Good night."

Liliane turned and walked into the lobby. She looked slim, taut, and entirely alone.

Watching her, I felt a wrench of unhappiness so intense my muscles contracted against it. I turned hurriedly away from the sight of her walking that way, alone, into that lobby, empty.

I started back through the tree-hung, reverberating streets toward the Gilded Pine. About halfway there I remembered: the Arab.

I had left a penniless, unknown Arab alone in my apartment.

Well, you had to be robbed at least once on the Riviera. I immediately realized what was most valuable there—a dwindling but still fairly thick roll of traveler's checks, certain clothes, the typewriter, a camera . . . the keys to the car. The beautiful blue Italian racer I couldn't even afford to own. I began walking fast. Maybe he didn't know how to drive. If he found and took all these things I would have to leave the Riviera; I would have to go back to Paris and work, "cured" or not. I would have to go back to the U.S.A. I hope they bring you more luck, checks and clothes and car, than they did me. I hope they bring you some luck. I crossed the terrace and went quickly into the apartment and up the curving marble stairs, flight after flight, being sure that a thief would come down the stairs and not in the elevator. I got to my door, listened, heard nothing, unlocked it, and went in. The light in the bathroom was on. I heard a low voice, and went to the bathroom door.

Jeannot the Arab was on his hands and knees, scrubbing the bathroom floor and singing faintly to himself.

He turned and looked at me over his shoulder, smiling almost shyly. "A little dirty, this floor. You noticed? But what's the matter? Did you meet an Algerian terrorist in the street? What a look you have! I know; she hit you with *her* frying pan, true? You look worse than this floor. I must wash you afterward, perhaps, no?"

I leaned against the doorjamb and looked philosophically at him. "Stop asking such direct questions; it isn't polite," falling myself into the friendly French singular.

"Ah, yes, that's true," he said soberly, and turned back to his energetic scrubbing. I just kept watching him. He continued scrubbing but turned a little so that out of the corner of his eye he could just make me out. He began to get self-conscious at the work. "I am going to finish this and then . . ." coming reluctantly to the point, "then I'm going to leave. Of course," more to himself, "I'm going to leave."

I went into the bedroom and sat down on the bed. I was tired and had a right to be tired. I stretched out and tried to think over what had happened to me that day, but almost immediately my mind began to stick on some detail—Liliane in pink, the little flaring gas jets of the stove, the glow of her pink clothes, the yellow-white-blue silent jets of flame, glowing pink, yellow, and white flame . . . Why didn't the Arab finish and go? . . . pay him something . . . pink . . .

I began to dream, some seemingly aimless dream about a parachute caught in a tree, the very white canopy of the chute. I couldn't pull it free; the harder I pulled, the tighter the harness became around my waist; I kept pulling harder and harder on that great white sheet caught in the prickly tropical tree, and the pain of the harness belt around my waist grew worse and worse. I *had* to get it free or else this terrific pain—

I woke up, stunned. My stomach. I was going to be very sick. Very sick. My head felt as though there was too much oxygen inside it, my stomach like some organism I would have to get rid of to live. I put a foot down on the floor, stepping on something smooth—a person, asleep, the Arab—stumbled over him through the darkened apartment, and just inside the bathroom door I began to vomit on the floor. I staggered on to the toilet. A minute later I felt a hand on my forehead, an arm around my chest.

Then he wiped me off with a damp cloth. I stumbled back to the bed. "Happy you're here," I mumbled, "very sick . . . don't know why."

"Sleep," he said in a low voice. "I will stay with you."

I was glad of that. I must have dozed for a little while, and then I began to tremble and the atmosphere inside my head thickened and the exhausting upheavals in my stomach began. I lurched out of bed, stepping on him again. "Bathroom . . ." He came with me.

At the end of that time I had less strength than before, and could not have got back to bed without him. But in my bleariness, perhaps it was even a delirium, I still noticed that the bathroom had been scrubbed clean again.

I lay in bed for a while, breathing deeply, shuddering, and then more or less dozed. But it didn't last. My insides began to rise; there was no possibility of anything there, but the upheaval began. This time the Arab was awake, sitting on the floor beside the bed. He took my arm and head and together we went into the clean bathroom.

At last the convulsions slowly receded and disappeared, and I lay sweating and unseeing and all but unconscious on the bed.

Must have polio, I thought to myself; must have eaten rat poison. Dimly I questioned the dinner the Arab had prepared; by accident or on purpose there might have been something poisonous in it. Arabs were great poisoners, weren't they? Or was that the Italians? I didn't care if he had done it, accidentally or on purpose. I was in his power now, and the one thing I asked was that he not leave, not now. Take everything later, take the car, only stay with me until I at least have the strength to hold the line again between being awake and being in a daze.

I began to lose it, began to sink back into a miasma of illusions. Don't leave me now. Steal everything later. Don't leave me alone here sinking. No wonder Liliane made love to others; it was a guarantee against being left alone. Aloneness was the most horrible state in the world; I saw that now. Better live with a sadist, a maniac, an imbecile. I understood that now, and this time I really and truly forgave her. I forgive you; I understand and I forgive you. The Arab stirred, standing near the open window, where morning was just beginning to gather. The movement drew me back toward awareness again. "What are you doing?" I said thickly. "Are you going to . . ."

"What?" he said softly.

"Nothing."

"Do you want something? Some water, for example?"

"No. God. No, nothing. But will you be able to stay for still a little while?"

"Oh, *yes*," in a reassuring, low voice, "yes."

"That's all," I murmured.

"You don't want to be alone," he said quietly; "it's that."

I took a deep breath and said, "Yes, I fear that most."

76

"It's natural," he said in his low voice, turning to look out the window. "Sleep. In the morning it will be better."

And with the morning beginning its dim signals in the sky behind him, I turned over and fell quickly into a motionless sleep.

When I awoke at about ten o'clock in the morning I realized two things at once: I was still so drained by sickness that I doubted whether I could stand, and I was intolerably hungry. There was no sound in the apartment, although there were the usual street rattles below. I had to eat but I couldn't get up. "Ah—" what was his name? "Gerard!" No. "Jeannot!"

There was no answer.

Well, of course this time he had done it. Feverishly I grasped it all. He had poisoned me—that strange taste in the omelet (Liliane must be lying helpless like this too)—and then he had calmly and coolly waited until the very last, when I was in the deepest sleep, to take everything. Smart young Arab. I couldn't see my camera or money or car or anything. They weren't normally visible from the bed, but that didn't mean anything. I had strength enough to get angry now, fever enough to get burningly angry. But even stronger than anger was one ruling demand: I had to eat. I felt sure that I would lose consciousness again and might never fully regain it if I didn't put something into my stomach. I hadn't the strength to stay conscious for long without nourishment, I felt sure of that. What was there to do? If only this apartment had a telephone!

I took several deep breaths, trying to calm myself, to think clearly, but they only made me dizzy. I had to make a plan. Otherwise I might really be in danger of being trapped here very sick for a long time. First I would try to get up and get to the kitchen and eat or drink something. Almost everything I could think of that was likely to be there revolted me, but I would try to find something. If I couldn't get up I would bang on the wall—no, this was an outside wall; no one would hear. Then, all right, I would begin to throw things through the window—I was good at that.

While I was still thinking, sweating, and shivering there in bed

I heard a wonderful noise, a delivering rattle, a great little commotion: someone was trying to put a key into the door of the apartment. Whoever it was kept turning the lock the wrong way—please don't give up trying—then I heard the lock turn the right way; there was a decisive click and the door could be heard opening. Someone came softly to the bedroom. It was the Arab. He raised his black eyebrows: "Well, you are not dead after all!"

"No," I said, trying for firmness but sounding weak even to myself.

"I thought you were going to die," he said straightforwardly.

"Me?" I tried a laugh. "I had only a sick stomach."

He smiled fully, but whether sincerely or not I couldn't tell. "You are better, then?"

"Ah, yes," I said not too convincingly, "yes."

"That's good. You would like to get up?"

"Get up? Perhaps not right away. Perhaps not."

"It doesn't surprise me. If it had been me, I would be dead. What a noise you made! Wait, take my hand." I took his hand, which was strong. "Squeeze! As hard as you can. Harder. That's as hard as you can squeeze? That's nothing. You are feeble as a child still." He gazed frowning at me.

"No, no, I feel much better."

". . . as a child."

In that instant, I don't know why, I decided to trust Jeannot. He had had a perfect opportunity to rob me and he had not done it. I still couldn't see my traveler's checks and camera and car, but I could feel them. I knew they were there. And I could hear them. I heard them in the straightforward tones of his voice.

"Listen, Jeannot. Come here. You know, you are right. I need somebody to work here. A comrade, I mean, as you said. A comrade to work here."

I said it simply; it seemed a simple, small announcement.

But Jeannot's whole being was transformed.

"It's true!" he said intensely, eyes narrowing with passion; "it's true!"

"You are my comrade here, beginning now, or rather last night."

He stood still for a moment, and then in a quiet, thoughtful voice, he said, "Thank God."

"What?" I said, my voice weak and shaking.

"Nothing," he said, shaking his head a little.

"You've had no work for a long time."

He shook his head.

"No money."

He shook his head again, peering at his feet.

"Well, well, that's finished now. Finished. No, no, look. You aren't going to cry—no, don't cry. Of course you will work here, for a long time. Me, you know, I am so badly organized, you can't realize how much I need someone. It's true! I can't do anything. I can't make coffee. How do you make coffee? It's with a . . . a frying pan, no? But after last night, I don't know. . . ."

He laughed, his head rolling back, a glimpse of white teeth and of tears, "The frying pan," he said chokingly.

I remembered a conversation when the De la Croies and Lili had talked about the impassivity of Arabs. I supposed people do show an impassive face when they feel hostility looking at them.

Jeannot, his face contorted with relief and tears, said, "I begin right now."

||||||||||||||||||||||

Juan-les-Pins entered the climax of the Grand Season: hot August came. People were wedged thigh to thigh the length of the riotous beach; night clubs bloomed everywhere, music pouring from hidden terraces and holes in the wall and basements; Sergio's mother moved into a cleaned-out chicken coop so that she could rent her bedroom at the exorbitant August rate. At the casino one gala followed another, luring the rich from behind their villa walls at Cap d'Antibes. The stray people appeared: bearded wandering youths from the North, with homemade shoes and no identity papers, en route around the world or to a war; a large young woman who went to all the night clubs and refused any invitations to dance so that she could dance by herself; a very old lady with a very young hairdo wearing furs and huge jewels who watched everything night and day through dark glasses with jeweled frames and by the end of the month was selling orangeade in a snack bar; a fine young man with a fine old title of nobility who was arrested at the end of the month for dealing in illicit drugs; a heroic movie star looking lost and ill; a Jamaican anthropologist just out of the jungle who began giving dancing lessons in a cabaret. They were not exceptions at Juan-les-Pins; they were part of the rule. The rule in hot August was to take courage from the streaming sunshine and to make that desperate try; whatever the impossible dream was that you had been nursing, now was the time to expose it, make that monumental bid, place that impossible bet, plunge at that chance for the brilliant career or liaison or crime. After August, in the words the men at the roulette tables repeated ritually at every spin of the wheel, nothing any longer went. Place your bets now, gentlemen-ladies. Everybody did.

||||||||||||||||||||

It took me nearly a week to recover from my sickness. During those days, as I took the careful nourishment Jeannot brought—from infusions and tea to clear soups and milk and fruit and finally vegetables and meat—I felt myself not only getting strong again but also cleansed, purged; I felt younger and healthier, as though I had delivered up the odds and ends of a hundred ill-considered French meals and also the odds and ends of a thousand ill-understood feelings, leftover emotions, the accumulated, indigestible shreds of experience that had been burdening me at Juan-les-Pins. My eyes and skin were clear; I felt a release of new energy. I felt more innocent, even, and a little worthier, a little more deserving of what most people would think of as vast good fortune, a season of irresponsibility on the French Riviera. It wouldn't last, of course, but that was all right; nothing lasted.

I felt almost as though now I was going to smash the great obscenity that kept Liliane from me. I didn't know how; I just felt that in this new worthiness born of sickness I was going to be able to do it.

Where was she? There was that cloud over me—there was no other cloud anywhere; we had entered one of those segments of summer in the South of France when the sky and the air were so flawlessly clear that everything moved closer together to celebrate; the Alps came forward from behind Nice and hung just beyond the next building; the old jumbled orange-roofed town of Antibes sat on its walled-in promontory and assaulted the observer's eye, thrusting its cubism and its colors, moving toward you if you looked at it for any length of time, each building separating itself from the surrounding jumble to display its lines and colors and vases of flowers; clotheslines arched separately, windows asserted their definite dimensions, roofs tilted in orange force—not enough tilt? they tilted a little more for you—everything to be seen acclaimed its particular shade and its individual shape, everything was beautiful, and everything was separate.

And Lili? She didn't answer the note I sent by Jeannot to her hotel. In fact she didn't seem to be there. I couldn't make out where she was, but in any case, as I pointed out to Jeannot when he came back from his last fruitless search, tomorrow I would be able to go out and find her myself. If God wished it, he added.

The following morning—in every detail identical with the preceding mornings, a chain of matching mornings of pure clarity and motionlessness—I went out into the street, where all the colors were washed and shining and separate, and walked through the celebrating shine of everything, including a huge red Esso gasoline truck stopped at an intersection waiting to be immortalized.

You do not find people at Juan-les-Pins in August. The only hope is that you may stumble over them. I walked the length of the beach twice and failed to stumble over her. Then I lay on a mattress for an hour but she didn't stumble over me.

Jimmy did. "Nick! I'm buying a car."

"You are? You haven't seen Lili, have you?"

"Lili? No."

"What kind of car are you buying?"

"That's just it. I don't know. What do you think?"

"I don't know, Jimmy; people have their own ideas about cars. What does Josée think, or is she still—"

"Josée's leaving it to me, as usual. Josée leaves *everything* to me, if you want to know the truth. That's what a man's for, she thinks. She thinks she's *flattering* me, for heaven sakes, when she asks me to decide everything we're going to do, and when, and where. I'm nervous, I'm a high-strung person—I know you've seen that in me—and I'm not used to being *taxed* like this. Taxed. Does Liliane tax you, Nick?"

"No. Yes. I don't know."

"She taxes me. And it's going to take us twice as long to get out of this country if I have to do it all. I try to explain to her that in America marriage is a partnership; we share; but she just smiles and lowers her eyes and *submits!* It makes me nervous, Nick. As though this war going on around here wasn't bad enough. I've got to get Josée's papers; I've got to get our passage; I've got to get a car—"

"What about that Porsche? You've got a car."

"It's used, Nick. I got that car nearly—I don't know, months ago. I don't want to bring a *used* car home to America. All that trouble getting it there and it's already half worn out. That wouldn't do. Come on up to the street with me. You don't have to go to showrooms here to pick out a car; you can just stand on a corner and *look!*"

We walked up to the street and stopped under a big palm tree; we watched the cars go by, creep by in the clogged traffic: swaying luxurious mammoths from the United States colored like candy boxes; cool British museums that seemed to lean away from the car in front; hot Italian numbers that leaned toward it; French oddities ignoring everybody else's tastes; rolling German powerhouses; light little white cars from Sweden; and then certain denationalized ones, unidentifiable special creations: a low-slung silver torpedo gliding forward on wire wheels; a sweeping, operatic-vintage touring car with flamboyant fenders; a gun-metal-gray combat wagon with a black leather interior and a green leather roof and a special searchlight in the middle of the grill like a single powerful eye; a Buick out of the thirties that had gone continental with silver horns on each fender and a leather trunk in the rear; little half-bicycle cars; and one perfect Rolls-Royce.

"You see what I mean, Nick. It's hard to choose."

"Yes." Three times I had thought I saw Lili in passing cars, but I was wrong.

"But I'm going to. I'm going to make up my mind, I am, I'm going to. And then I'm—we're leaving. Because, you know something, Nick? Even if there wasn't this war going on around here, and the people getting knifed and all that, I still wouldn't want to stay. The thing is, when you get right down to it, there's not too much to *do* around here; did you ever notice that? Josée doesn't think so. She thinks there's plenty to do. But what? I ask you, what?"

"Well, what did you do in Ardmore?"

"Work, Nick," he said, not convincingly, "work."

"What else besides that?"

"I don't know, I forget, something. There was always something to do. Here, I don't know. . . ." He was silent; then he looked at his watch. "It's stopped; it must be almost time for lunch. The Victory. Do you know what, Nick? I'm tired of the Victory. Tired of the Victory? I'm tired of lunch." His eyes followed a passing Aston-Martin. "How do you spend your time, anyway?"

"For the past week I've been spending it in bed. I was sick."

"Oh. But what do you do usually?"

"There always seems to be something to do. Right now I'm looking for Liliane. You haven't—but you said you hadn't, didn't you?"

"What else do you do?"

After a moment I replied, "I suffer."

He looked at me, took his time about deciding how to take that, and then decided I was joking. " 'I suffer.' That's good, Nick. I'm going to use that. That's funny, that really is." And after another pause—these pauses indicated more than anything else how unhappy he was that day—he added, "But you know something? It's not just funny. It's true." He looked vacantly in front of him, mouth slightly open, and then he said, in a strange mumble I did not recognize, "I do suffer." He turned his eyes, under the bulge of his receding forehead with a naked look toward me, "I wonder why," he added in the same voice. "I always suffered, and I never knew why." His naked eyes searched for something in my face. "Did you?"

"Never in time," I said.

"I never knew why. I don't know now, either. It's funny, to suffer here."

We stood watching the cars go by for a little longer and then I started off. "Goodbye, Jimmy."

"Goodbye," he said, letting me take my leave for the first time without wanting to hold me or to arrange a meeting soon. He stood thinking beneath the big palm tree as the procession of cars moved slowly past.

I went back to my apartment for lunch. From the bathroom I heard a faint, abstracted crooning:

> *Gondolier, do you remember?*
> *Gondolier, under the blue sky*
> *You were singing*
> *A song so be-au-ti-ful . . .*

The high, sliding notes here were a little too much for Jeannot's voice; he had to strain like a young boy singing, but he just managed to stay on key. He didn't know anyone was listening, and his voice wasn't up to it, but his feelings seemed to be. He sang softly and earnestly, wanting to get that song out, to express the feelings he had, to make something nice somehow:

> *Gondolier, when you were singing—*
> *La, de da da DA da*

Da de da DA *da*
Da da . . .

I went to the bathroom door. He stood in a pair of white shorts, his legs straight, bending from the waist over the bathtub, washing something out.

"What's that?" I asked.

"A shirt. I have to keep it clean."

"No, I mean that song."

"I don't know. I sing to pass the time. I have many songs. I am going to show you later." He went on scrubbing, hard but carefully. It was his good shirt, white. And when I went into the other room he slowly tuned up the song again, slowly and unconsciously; it seemed to go with the scrubbing.

In the corner of the living room were two suitcases I had never seen before.

"Jeannot!"

"Yes?"

"Nothing—"

I sat down, pretending that I hadn't seen the suitcases. After a while he came in, the white shirt carefully draped over a hanger that he put to dry on a knob of the glass door opening on the balcony.

"How is that room of yours in Antibes?"

"That room? All right. If I understand which room you mean."

"I mean the one you're living in, in Antibes."

"Oh. That one." He was having trouble making the damp sleeves fall in just the way he wanted.

"Well?"

"Yes?"

"Well, do you like the room you're living in?"

"That is to say, I'm not altogether living there, isn't that true? Now I'm here," he said definitely, "during the day."

"But it's all right there at night, when you go home to sleep?"

"That's all right," he said, opening the glass doors wide for better ventilation of the shirt. "That's all right." He came back into the room. "You haven't noticed what I brought, to celebrate your recovery."

Those two battered suitcases? "You mean those—" I said, starting to point.

"The flowers! Look!" There was a pitcher stuffed with brilliant blossoms on a small table near the balcony.

"Nice."

"One hundred francs. She wanted three hundred. I was looking at them all the time saying No; I wasn't going to buy anything, but I came back from time to time because it was getting close to noon and she was afraid she wasn't going to sell them at all. So at last she sold them to me for one hundred francs. Smell them. Very strong smell."

I didn't have to get up to smell them because now I became aware of a fragrance hanging in the air of the room.

"But those two suitcases. They aren't a present too?"

"Those?" His glance at them implied that they were contemptible, unimportant items not worth noticing. "A few belongings . . ." He inhaled deeply. "What fragrance!"

"What kind of belongings? Clothes?"

A preoccupied nod.

"Your clothes?"

Another nod. "I wanted to put them in order. I brought them to arrange in free moments today. That doesn't bother you?"

"No, of course not."

Now that I had torn an explanation of the valises out of him, he felt free to deal with them. "Those bastards, the police. Look at that!" He indicated a long gash in the better-looking of the two cases, a fairly good-looking one until I got closer and saw that it was made of a material like cardboard. There was a slit almost the length of one side.

"The police did that?"

"Yes," he said, nodding grimly, "the cops. I was in Paris working, but then I didn't want to stay, because the F.L.N.—you understand what that means, the F.L.N.? They are the Moslem chiefs of the rebellion against the French in Algeria—they were always bothering me in Paris. They are too strong there. Pay this, they said; contribute to that, do this. Me, I don't give a damn for politics. I got fed up with the F.L.N. 'You are Algerian,' they said all the time. 'You must fight or you must pay.' I wanted to work, that was all. So I decided to get out of Paris before I lost my temper, with them or with the police. I got out. I came here, where I was before. Here they—here I am"—his face brightened almost nostalgically, "well loved. Yes," he said this valuable word again, softly, "well loved by people who know me. It's true. The French here are all right to me. It's more peaceful here, too. But you see, I had to get out of Paris very fast. The two of them—the F.L.N. and the police—*both* were chasing me!" He looked with a sudden surprised smile at me. "It was simple; I had to choose or risk being killed, or maybe just put in jail." Then he added more mildly: "I don't want to choose. I am myself, that's all. I'm not a rebel. I like the French. I, do you know, I love France. Yes. I ran the risk of saying that some day to the F.L.N., in their teeth. So I got out of Paris. But so fast I left my two bags. My cousin sent them to me. The police looked at the name —my Arab name—and they took a razor, and *trrack!* slit the side of the bag like that. They were looking for bombs, perhaps, or a machine gun"—his eyes brightened—"and they found dirty laundry!"

He now felt comfortable enough with the suitcases to go over to them. "Let's see." He opened the slashed one, putting his fingers meditatively along the gap, studying it with a kind of slow incredulity, and an expression on his face that said, "I know this is true, but still, how can this have happened?" Then he opened the suitcase.

Inside, everything was neatly packed. There were several undershirts and shorts, two pairs of work pants, carefully mended; a pair of Mediterranean sandals, three elegant neckties, a packet of letters and some snapshots. He handed me one. "Photo of my father."

His father wore a hooded robe, and had a short white beard. The only resemblance to Jeannot I could see was a certain open expression on his face. This is me myself, the expression seemed to say. I am myself, I am what you see, nothing more, nothing less. But it was this expression of Jeannot's, deepened and dignified by age, filled out by many tests of its integrity, and not found wanting. If Jeannot's habitual expression conveyed "I am myself," his father's conveyed "I have been myself for a long time in spite of everything."

"He is well loved," Jeannot said slowly.

"Yes, I can believe it." I handed back the photograph. "Is your family all right these days?"

"Ah, how is anybody these days in Algeria?"

He lifted out a summer shirt, quite small, almost a boy's shirt. It too had been mended. He held it doubtfully across his chest. When he bought that shirt he must have been practically a boy himself. Could it still be worn? He considered this tranquilly to himself, and apparently deciding the attempt was at least worth making, folded it and put it beside him on the floor. His strong hands handled all the individual bits of clothing in the suitcase with deference, slowly picking them up and sorting them out, thinking over each pair of underpants, every sock. There were a couple of towels, a washcloth shaped like a mitten, a bed sheet, even a few sheets of toilet paper in the valise.

"Look at this!" He held up what seemed to be a small bit of leopard skin.

"What is it?"

"Bathing suit." He held it against himself. It was the irreducible minimum in swimming trunks. "To walk on the beach!"

"Sensational."

"Isn't it? Ah. Another photo. Of me, this time."

The snapshot showed him with two desert Arabs in full robes, standing in the sand. He himself wore pants and a hat tilted on one side; it looked like a Spanish dancer's hat, with a large straight brim and a flat crown. He looked slim, almost debonair, not at all like the sheik of the movie fantasy but still like the young heir of some landowner, the well-off young blood, chaperoned by two of his father's servants in the desert.

"On a ranch. South of Oran. My father raised cattle there. But not now."

Everything having to do with Algeria came to this kind of inconclusive stop or suspension in his conversation: his father raised cattle, but no longer; his brother lived in such-and-such a place, but not now; cafés for dancing had a certain kind of music, that is, they used to; healers used certain herbs for illness, or had when the herbs were available; the best hotels were in this town and at that beach, if they were open now; in his father's house guests stayed in this particular room, or had stayed in it when there were guests; a younger brother studied in a particular school, only not now; the weather was of a special type at this time of year, but this year, well, perhaps it was different. Nothing could be said with certainty about Algeria any more; it was like a patient in the crisis of a disease. Still, he kept returning to the subject, had to talk about it, it seemed—about "at home"—and I promised that Yes, I would visit him; yes, I would see it all; yes, yes, we would ride south into the desert on his father's horses. Later, when it was as it had been.

Now Algeria could only be talked about—and so we talked about it, just as all the newspapers and radio stations and politicians and everyone else in France did, for the contagion had touched France too; France was a little feverish herself, France too was suffering; the two invalids lay in different states of illness across the Mediterranean from each other, and the famous sea glittered between, transparent, very blue, very peaceful. There we swam every day, day after unchanging day, and noticed the soldiers slowly accumulating.

Liliane had disappeared. She had disappeared from my life, although I might easily have passed within ten yards of her every day. The crowd was too overpoweringly thick; if you once broke hands with someone, once failed to keep a rendezvous, your friend might be swept off and away, never to be found again. Somewhere out of sight Max and Mireille and the others I used to see every day probably struggled ahead as before. I didn't see them.

Liliane had left her hotel without leaving a forwarding address.

She had, however, left baggage there, so at least I knew that some time she would come back. Apparently she left the morning after the frying-pan dinner at my apartment. She had left, of course, thinking that that was what I wanted her to do.

I went to the De la Croies. They were away, cruising on a chartered yacht. And that, of course, was where Liliane was.

I did run into Mireille one night in front of Pam-Pam. Her only news was that there were "diseases in the sand of the beach." All the bodies lying side by side, sweating and spitting, she said, and spilling drinks and lotion and putting out cigarettes, returned after all this had been raked into the same thin layer of sand and lay down on it again, day after day. By this time of year the germs were reinforced and concentrated; an epidemic of something might break out at any time. Not to mention the danger of skin diseases. As for the water in front of the beach . . .

But then she saw someone else and the crowd heaved and we were washed apart and I never learned what peril the water itself held in August.

The one old acquaintance I did see regularly was Sergio, since he was always at the Victory. The pressure of August seemed to be strongest on Sergio. Every day he talked a little faster, his eyes darted more quickly, his laughter came more often and more abstractedly. "Nice day, ha-ha-ha," he would say; "And what can I bring you, ha-ha-ha?" or, "You swam, ha-ha-ha?"

He no longer watched me closely to see that I didn't interfere between Jimmy and Josée. He didn't seem even to be watching them closely. He was watching, all right, watching harder and more sharply than ever, but not us. He was watching the street, or the sky, or perhaps the stock market, or perhaps himself. This new watching was more concentrated than ever, and combined with the harried pace of business in August and his own drive to establish himself before his wedding, it seemed to me that Sergio was on the edge of breaking apart.

"You'd better take a few days off," I finally said to him one day after he spilled a drink and broke the saucer and cut himself picking it up, "you'd better rest. You can't get married in this state."

"I know, I know," he breathed to himself, and dashed away to another table. One of the other waiters, who'd been helping him pick up the pieces, turned, however, his face drawn and as pale as in Finland in February, and said: "When can any one rest? We start at seven in the morning. We quit at eleven at night, if we're lucky. We work seven days a week. When can we rest? But you are right. We are not machines."

The next day, when I came to the Victory, Sergio beckoned me into the kitchen. We went to his retreat among the wine bottles. "Nick, what you said yesterday was true, very true. But you understand the problem. I have no money. I will be paid only at the end of the month. Could you, a little loan, say"—gathering his courage —"thirty thousand francs," and instantly noting a flicker of reaction on my face, "twenty thousand, even ten. I have to have a little money. I beg you. For an old friend." He tried to smile, an alarming try. "We are almost brothers, no?"

I had to tell him that I was living on credit myself, and credit was as hard to find at Juan-les-Pins as silence, or space.

He immediately dropped the question, not angrily or even regretfully; he simply discarded it. Things were too pressing to take time for anger or regret.

I went out into the powerful sunshine and walked the few blocks to my car. Jeannot was waiting for me in it; we were going to drive together to Old Antibes to pick up a few remaining clothes there. "I want to profit from your apartment to wash all my things," he said.

Since it was noontime, driving happened to be easy; France was at lunch. We went along the wall-enclosed Way of the Sands, cutting across the miniature peninsula of Cap d'Antibes, and glided down into the Old Town.

"Beautiful day," he murmured as we passed into the planes and tilts and pastels of the place, the flowers stuck here and there in stray crevices, the shutters and lanes, the precarious vases and bits of bas-relief over hovel doorways, crumbling walls and wine caves, stairways going up and over and through and ending in space, the clammy basements and leaking roofs and glassless windows and poisonous restaurants and poverty and crooks and water of Old Antibes.

"Yes, it is a beautiful day. You said you knew a lot of songs. Sing."

I looked at him for a moment, in the eyes. They weren't black, I saw in the absolute clarity of the light, but a very dark brown, filled now with an expression of indecision. "I can't sing," he said.

"Of course you can. I heard you."

"That's nothing; that's to amuse myself."

"You know many songs. You said you had copies of the music."

"Oh, I got those for myself, to sing to myself, in my room at night." A long pause; since I didn't ask him to go on he did so voluntarily. "It's very active here in the summer, but in the winter it's completely another thing. I sing in the winter in the evenings, in my room, to myself." Then he added quietly, letting the truth come out—the truth eventually always came out of Jeannot, filtered out slowly, like sand—"when I had a room." So there it was; the two suitcases, one of them slit, were home.

"You sang in your room in the winter, just for yourself?"

"Sure. It passes the time. If not, one could be sad here in the winter, very sad."

We came to an alley too narrow even for this miniature car, and so we went to the end of it on foot, and into a slab of an old house, stone-floored, dark, a house half-open to the weather, up a stony passage with the sky coming through big stone apertures here and there, up to the top of the house, where we entered a kind of cement shed stuck under the roof with a ceiling so slanted that we could stand only in the higher part of the room, next to the bed. A light bulb jutted out of the wall over the bed. "I sat here in bed and sang. There was a light then so I could see the music."

"Yes, I see."

"Do you see?"

"Yes."

"It's all right; it's not bad."

"No."

"I was okay here. I was all right."

"Yes."

"Why do you have that funny expression on your face? It was comfortable enough here, I tell you. I didn't suffer."

"No, no, of course, yes." I looked hurriedly around the room. "What's that? Is that yours?" The only other thing in the room besides the bed and a rickety table was a small cardboard box.

"Ah, yes, that's it. The concierge left it here, since she hasn't rented the room yet to someone else." He picked up the box and put it on the table. With the appreciative slowness I had noticed before in his hands, he lifted out a sheaf of sheet music. "Here they are."

They were the popular French favorites of the past few years, *La Vie en Rose* and *La Mer* and *La Seine* and *Donne-moi* and *Rossignol* and *Mes Mains* and *Gondolier,* the sentimental ones, the pretty and a little heartfelt ones, the ones a person alone might sing like lullabies to himself.

"Sing one of them now," I said.

He looked slowly and carefully at me. "I can't sing," he murmured.

"As if I were not here."

He sat down on the pile of bed, holding the music. Then he leaned back against the wall and opened one of the sheets of music. His eyes explored it carefully, wondering. Then in his low voice he tentatively began:

> *The sea*
> *That you watch dancing along the bright bays*
> *Makes silver shimmers,*

The sea
Makes changing shimmers
Under the rain.

"That was the way you sang—that was good, Jeannot—in the winter to pass the evening. That was good."

"Better than being on the street. Every light in Antibes goes out at nine o'clock on winter evenings. It's not gay."

"That—I liked that"—he could hardly sing at all—"in the winter by yourself like that—you were here by yourself, singing. Well, you'll see, next winter will be better; you will be able to go home to Algeria; this war will be over. You're going to see. It'll be all right; and then you can go home and not spend the winter alone like that, like this, in this room. Not like this at all. You'll see."

He listened patiently and watchfully with a distant little smile on his face, and then he picked up the box and we went down the sloping passage that spilled us out into the alley.

Opposite the doorway a faucet with a lion's head for a spigot dripped a thin line of water into a little stone basin. At the end of the alley, near where I had left the car, there was a more ambitious watering place, a small fountain with an obelisk in the center. We got into the car and drove down a narrow street. Wedged amid a clutter of leaning old houses was a large shed under which a wide current of water continually flowed along a concrete trough: women did their washing there, standing in a pit within the U-shaped trough of flowing water. Water could be heard rushing through pipes attached to the outside of houses. There was another fountain, quite large, with statues crouching under a spray of water that flowed over them into subsidiary basins before disappearing. In a recess in the town wall was another large shed through which water coursed in a trough. We drove through the arch in the wall and out into the Port of Antibes, where the harbor was enclosed by a long white wall of Roman arches ending in a small tower, and beyond this wall was the open sea, as though all the water spurting and flowing and spraying throughout the town had been woven into it from this surrounding sea.

"What's that in your hand?" I asked as we circled the port.

"Biscuit crumbs," he said. "I found them in the bottom of the box. When we get back to our—the apartment, I will put them out on the balcony," he looked complacently in front of him, "for the little birds."

The little birds. In the end I realized that the little birds were almost as significant to Jeannot as the Algerian war. They were a part of his vision of the world, of his scale of values, of his sense of responsibility. Often he would interrupt himself in the most unlikely places to feed or just look at or merely wonder about the little birds. Never just the birds: always the little birds. "It is a good day for the little birds," he would say in the morning. "I'm going to save that," he might say, taking some poor scrap of food found on the tablecloth at the end of a meal, "for the little birds." He disapproved of the heavy winds that sometimes caromed around the Riviera because they were "not good for the little birds."

There was something fragile and something gentle about birds that excited his sympathy: He was strong and they were under his care, or perhaps, in a country where he was considered at the same time a Frenchman with full rights and a terrorist enemy alien, he turned to these creatures he could protect, who were more vulnerable than he was. He didn't know birds, couldn't tell one species from another, had no idea of their habits or what they liked to eat or where they were going or where they had been. He just put out crumbs for them and thought repeatedly about them, frail and sailing around up there, hungrily, and so small always, so alone: the little birds.

I turned up the hill away from the port and climbed to the Place de Gaulle, where the chaos of traffic made it clear that the French nation had finished its lunch. Jeannot kept sinking lower in his seat. I continued making my way very slowly behind the traffic around the square. He seemed to want almost to hide, which was impossible in this low open car; if we were riding forward on a platter we could not have been more visible.

"What's the matter with you?" I said.

"Nothing," he answered vaguely, "tired."

We crept on, Jeannot growing more and more uneasy.

"Is there anything the matter?"

"No . . . nothing."

He slid into different positions, and several times seemed on the point of springing out of the car. At last we reached the exit from the square, the Boulevard the President Wilson; the traffic cleared, and we drove on quickly to Juan-les-Pins.

When we got to the apartment Jeannot went straight to the balcony and scattered the crumbs conveniently here and there. Then he searched the sky for a minute or two, as though signaling. Finally, he came in and began fixing lunch. It reminded me of what I had been taught to do when I used to raise dogs: always feed the animals first.

Jeannot set the table near the open glass doors of the balcony, using a rented tablecloth and napkins, red and green, matching, cheerful. The immortal cut flowers he put in the center. "Wineglasses," that is, tumblers. A thin, tapering bottle of Provençal wine. The golden twist of bread, rinsed lettuce leaves, two hard-boiled eggs under a yellow sauce, a crisp flat fish, already boned, a garlicky, oniony potato salad, wild strawberries with thick cream and sugar, and a determined cup of coffee.

"Jeannot," my voice almost quavered, "that was totally delicious."

He smiled faintly, looking at the tablecloth. "By the way," I went on, "what's that you were putting on your food?"

It was a red sauce that he took on the end of his knife from a small can with a label in Arabic.

"Try some," he said, putting a speck on a piece of bread.

I tried it. My mouth burned quietly for half an hour afterward. He had been steadily eating it with his food in lumps. "You're from another world," I said when I could say something.

96

"It's good for love; that gives you force, you know."

"That's true? Then it's worth it, barely."

He glanced over at the balcony with silent pleasure; another little bird had come for lunch.

"Me," he then went on with a candid glance, "I'm always in form."

"In form for making love?"

"Yes."

"Bravo."

"Yes, it's in the blood. At home we make real love. Not like here. Over there," a sharp gesture of the head sideways, "we make real love."

"Yes, and you continue to do that when you come here, according to the newspaper. Did you read this story?" and I handed him the paper. The story described a young Algerian whose amorous involvement with a family for whom he worked included members of both sexes and two generations. A wild family quarrel in which two people were wounded had brought his affairs to light. Jeannot poured over the story, dark eyes widened as they always were when he read; slowly, intently, he made his way through it. Toward the end his mouth began to widen in a wry smile, and at the end he threw his head back and laughed explosively. "You notice," he cried breathlessly, "the one thing they didn't want to lose was *him!*"

"Yes, I noticed."

"Everything else kicked in the air! But each one wanted to keep him. Oh, my God, this story, what a howl! I've never read one like that till now," and he wiped his eyes.

"You're all sex maniacs."

"Yes!" nodding helplessly, his face contorted from glee at the complexity and truth of it all. Every kind of arrangement and relationship was possible. But calming down finally, he added: "But the poor guy. Caught, eh." A philosophic sigh. "It's like that. Nothing to be done. Still, he went too far. Four members of one family. I'm not surprised it ended badly. He went too far."

Late that afternoon he went out to buy some food for dinner. He was not back at six, or seven, or eight. Finally, he came in at about eight-thirty, with no food. "Well, where is it? What is there to eat? Why so late?"

He made his way to the balcony, muttering, "More crumbs for the little birds," and then turned on the radio. He sat down and put his elbows on his knees, examining his hands vacantly.

"What's the matter with you?"

He sighed slowly, blinked, and went on looking at his hands with their several old scars.

"Are you sick? What's the matter with you?"

He looked up finally. "Yes, sick." His eyes looked fixedly at me for a while, and then back at his hands. "Do you know where I passed the afternoon?"

"Of course not."

"At the police headquarters. That is why I am sick. Me, at the police headquarters. I never harmed a cat. Never." His eyes came up again, black now, his teeth clenched, and he suddenly exclaimed in a fierce voice, "On the head of my mother, *I never harmed anyone!*"

"Well, then—"

"They searched me. A detective went over me with his hands, even here." He grabbed his testicles. "When he did that I said, 'Fine goods, no?' Like that, in his face, 'Fine goods, no?' He said nothing, just searched."

"Why did—"

"He didn't find anything. Nothing to find. May God—may God take out my eyes, I am not a criminal! May I never see my father again, may my mother die in pain, I am *not a criminal!*"

"There is that rebellion."

"Politics! What do I know of politics! What is all that noise to

98

me! They search me, a man grabs my balls, because I am an Arab. What is your work? they say. What money have you? Whose car were you riding in today? Who is that other one? Questions! They search me, they grab me, 'Fine goods, no?' That's what I said. They're all a band of bastards. I want to get out of here. Take me to America, I beg you. This country is rotten. Take me out of here. I don't give a damn for politics. Yes, you are right, yes. I am sick."

Later I went out and had dinner in a restaurant near the Place de Gaulle. Although I offered to buy him dinner there, he refused, and went off by himself to a small place near the port. Later I saw him in an open bar. He was a little drunk, talking excitedly to another Arab, arguing. Two Arabs in argument is a sight to chill non-Mediterranean blood. Dark shapely face close to dark shapely face, they narrowed their eyes to Oriental slits, their faces becoming masks of bottomless hate, proud with a grandeur of evil, fingers pointing like bayonets, murderous asides, endless threatening grimaces, a concentrated lust for destruction blazing in both of them. Suddenly the argument broke; first the other Arab and then Jeannot became more casual and friendly with each other, almost suave, the ancient Mediterranean reversal: on the brink of a real fight they stopped. Both now knew all they needed to know about the other's feelings. So why fight? At least, why fight now, here? Smiles curved, voices turned reasonable, almost gay; the lights in their eyes receded, gestures became easier; a truce, a draw.

||||||||||||||||||||||

The next morning he was at my apartment scrupulously on time to fix my breakfast, which he served me in bed.

"I saw you last night," I said as he handed me a big cup of mixed strong coffee and hot milk, "and you were drunk."

His eyes darted in a disconcerted way here and there for a moment and then he pulled himself together and said stoutly, "Drunk? Me? No, I wasn't drunk."

"You were arguing with somebody in Arabic in that café down

the street and you were drunk. I saw you. You're not supposed to drink. You're a Moslem."

"I was *not* drunk. But not at all. Still, if I *wanted* to become drunk, I would do it. Why not? I don't have much pleasure. It doesn't do any harm." He handed me a *croissant*. "Did you notice the other one? Did he have the air of being drunk too, according to you?"

"Yes."

Smiling secretively, Jeannot moved around the room, rolling up the big louvered outer blind so that the sun moved steadily across the floor with its unwavering morning radiance, falling finally on my face like a faithful salute, as though it had been waiting patiently outside my window just to do this.

"He wasn't drunk," Jeannot continued; "he was drugged."

"Ah, well."

"Yes. Keef. He smokes it now and then. It's a bad idea, I don't approve of it."

"Yes."

"You haven't tried it? Shall I get some for you?"

"I thought you said it was very bad, and that you didn't approve of it."

"Yes, I said that. I don't like it myself. But *you*, you are another person, isn't that so?" He sat down in a chair with a self-possessed, inner-looking expression. "Perhaps it will please you, I don't know."

"No, I don't think it will. I think—it seems to me that it's a question of cultural expectation." When he heard the words "cultural expectation" pronounced by me in a certain tone of voice, his eyes glazed over, although he continued to listen with a form of blank attention. He had got to know that tone of voice. There was a lecture coming. I started in quickly and immediately—I hardly ever had a chance for a theoretical discussion on the Riviera—by pointing out that culturally it was unexpected for me to take drugs, just as it was culturally unexpected for him to drink. It was culturally more expected for him to take drugs. Jeannot was studying his prize possession, a gold-plated wrist watch, not the face but the back, where he found several miniscule scratches. I went on to say that our bodies were differently conditioned; that mine was conditioned to tolerate alcohol and his to tolerate drugs. Part of this conditioning came from our own habits and part from what our ancestors had done for many generations. "It's better to stay with the stimulants for which your body and your culture have conditioned you, no?" I wound up.

He looked up from the watch. "Did you say you wanted some keef?"

"Aren't you listening—"

"Yes, of course. You said that some people like keef and some people like alcohol. It's what I've already said myself. But do you want some keef, you?"

"*No!*"

"Oh. Then why didn't you simply say so?"

||||||||||||||||||||||||

That day I happened to run into Mireille near the beach. For the first time that summer she was without her dog, the thin little poodle she always took to the beach and the restaurants and all the night clubs. "Where is he?" I asked.

"The dog?" she said shortly. "Dead. He was never strong, you know; sickly. He died last week."

"He was a cute little thing."

"Yes." She was looking over my shoulder and here and there as we stood talking on the beach promenade with the crowd brushing past us, all the good-looking and almost naked young people sauntering against a background of tourists and families and middle-aged unmarried couples on a spree.

Mireille seemed very preoccupied, so much so that she couldn't focus her allure on me for once, but stood there in her over-tanned skin and little strips of bathing suit like a hesitating animal, either hunted or hunting, nervous but not despairing, extremely alert, concentrating, preoccupied. "Oh," she said. "I saw Liliane."

It took me a moment to absorb that, and then I asked, "Where did you see her?"

"At Villefranche. She was there on somebody's boat, cruising."

"Whose boat was it?"

Her attention wandering, "I don't know."

"Did you see the people she was with?"

"No. Or yes, I saw her with some people later in the street."

"Did you know any of those people, Mireille?"

"Uh—no, no."

"What did they look like? How many of them were there? Were there both men and women?"

"Four or five. Yes, men and women."

"You didn't know any of them."

Turning her head to follow with her eyes someone passing, "No, I didn't know them."

"Were they her age or older?"

"Different ages. I didn't pay very much attention. I didn't speak to them on the street. They were all talking together."

I looked at and through her and finally I said, "Having a good time together."

"It seemed. Very gay. Do you have a cigarette? Thanks. Oh, French ones. Never mind, I'll get some. I must go. The water-skiing preliminaries are going to start there beyond the casino. Coming?"

"No. Thanks, Mireille."

Leaving, she turned and added, "Liliane is coming back here, she mentioned. For some fête at the casino."

"Fête? Which fête? They have a fête almost every night at the casino. What fête?"

"I forget. For the army or the police or something. Some fête. Perhaps we'll meet on the beach later."

It was four weeks to the day since I had seen Liliane.

That afternoon I drove to the De la Croies' villa again. Yes, the housekeeper said, the family was still away. On the sea, taking a cruise.

There are two old sayings about the situation in which I found myself: "Out of sight out of mind" and "Absence makes the heart grow fonder." They are both very much quoted, for the reason that they are both so true, but one applies to one kind of person, the other to the other. I was the other. I longed for her with an intoxicated, half-conscious permanence, in a completely unreasonable, hypnotized trance, in the way, for instance, that exiled Frenchmen long for Paris. They may have been unhappy, underpaid, abused slaveys in Paris, and if they went back there they might be again. The romance and beauty and elegance of Paris had never been for them. It didn't matter. They were exiled; they were French. They longed for Paris.

People long for what uses them. That is why heaven seems so repulsive. People want to be committed, to have their minds and backs and fears and nerves seized and tested, wrecked if necessary, abused as a last resort. But not neglected, not stunted, not withering from disuse. Liliane had used my body and my feelings and my fury and my desire more than any woman ever had. It had not been pleasant, not pleasant at all, ever. Life was pleasant now. And that was why I longed permanently for her to come back.

Not that I forgave her. Whatever this "fire" fed on, I couldn't forgive her or myself for not having quenched it, all of it, even the part that went into her music. But I thought: I'm a little tougher now. I can take more now. I'll take it, I'll try it. Maybe I can do it. When I was sick those days I even forgave her, forgave her, until I got better. Of course, my forgiveness didn't last. But maybe it would eventually. And was there something I "withheld" from her? Whatever that might be, maybe I had it now.

That afternoon passed pleasantly on the beach. It was pack-jammed of course, but in order still, French, the rows of umbrellas and mattresses enforcing a certain symmetry, and although the water was bathtub warm and full of drifting blades of grass and seaweed, still it was the sea. It was not a magnificent day, not a stunning natural experience, not sublime; just pleasant. I knew which little segment of the beach Mireille frequented and so managed to find her. We lay on mattresses next to each other and I periodically returned to her encounter with Lili, returning to that every fifteen minutes or so with a new question on some detail, another query on what her impression of the people with Lili had been, for instance, until I was certain that I knew everything that she could possibly tell me. The only important fact in it all was that Liliane was coming back for some fête at the casino, sometime.

Mireille wished to discuss other people. "Your friend Sergio is disoriented," she said.

"In what way?"

"The police. It's all right, a little contraband now and then, but Sergio overdoes it! Four hundred thousand francs in one week, not to mention black-market dollars and the other affairs. He wants to be a millionaire by the time he marries. It's not possible."

"He hasn't been arrested, has he?"

"Ah, no, not that. But they're watching him," and Mireille looked balefully at me: surveillance. "They're watching. Sergio had better pay attention or else he will have his honeymoon at the state's expense." She looked past me. "There's the American, the one who's a spy. He's a slippery one, pretending to be so dumb. A true rascal."

"Jimmy?" turning to look and then turning back. "You don't still believe that spy story—" but Mireille merely intensified her habitual knowing expression, and then Jimmy was with us.

"Nick!" he said in his usual surprised tone. "Mireille!" as though he were running into us in Tokyo.

"Jimmy!" Mireille shot back.

"Here's Josée," he said, and Josée, sunburned instead of tanned, cautiously greeted us. Jimmy began to discuss the problems of the day: Would war break out before Josée got her papers to emigrate? Would he find the appropriate foreign car for Ardmore living? Would there be enough to do around here in the meantime? Would those expensive beach clothes go on sale before he left? Mireille was searching the beach and the passing crowd with her eyes, and I began to look around also, sure that Jimmy would carry on. Then, standing on the beach promenade behind and above us, I noticed Jeannot. He was looking down at me, and something in the calm, isolated atmosphere about him made me imagine that he had materialized there, suddenly, out of thin air. There was a trace of the jinni about Jeannot sometimes, an ability to appear and disappear inexplicably, an unlikely gift for knowing a little too much about certain things. He was wearing a rust or almost gold-colored sports shirt, and bright-blue Mediterranean pants. His black wavy hair shone in the sun. I had never used this part of the beach before, but I was not at all surprised that he had found me here. I had a feeling he could find anyone anywhere. He had not found Liliane, and that proved that she was not here, even before Mireille confirmed it.

I motioned for him to come down, but he backed away and shook his head almost sternly, glancing aside with a touch of nervousness. What was the matter with him? Acting like some kind of international bomb thrower here on a sunny afternoon at the beach! The police had questioned him; all right. They had searched him; that was no cataclysm either. "Come here a minute!" I yelled above the noise, causing Mireille and Jimmy to turn but leaving Josée staring vacantly into the sand as before. Across the twenty-five yards I saw Jeannot's eyes flare with some emotion, and then he backed away. Mireille and Jimmy, failing in a second to see who it was I had called to, lost interest and looked elsewhere. Jimmy went on talking—war, Ardmore, Josée, Aston Martin, clothes—and when I looked up at the beach promenade a couple of minutes later there was Jeannot, looking calmly down at me.

He would have stood there quietly all afternoon, which made him different from everyone else I knew at Juan-les-Pins. Time meant very little to him; he drifted indifferently ahead of schedule and behind schedule, if his life could be said to have anything as rigid as a schedule. He didn't quite grasp time, or making time count, or using time well. He lost track of time for long periods of it. He didn't care about goals, either; he invented and replaced and forgot them in a rapid shuffle of interests. He cared only about two things: his next meal and his sentiments. His sentiments began with himself and arched iridescently over into certain friends and most deeply, of course, into his own family. They did not include anything so abstract as patriotism, either French or Algerian. And they did include, naturally, the little birds. He stood on the beach promenade in his gold shirt gazing placidly down at me. He would not come down or even motion to me. He would just look at me, for as long as necessary.

I got up and picked my way across the flaunting bodies to the decorated stone steps and went up to him. As I approached, his face gradually came to a smile of mixed shyness and pleasure, something like a young fisherman's face when he lands a tough one that he's proud of. "Greetings," he said.

"Are you going for a swim?"

"No, I'm walking. I have to meet a—someone over there," chin jerking up to indicate the general direction, "later. Say. The lunch was good today, wasn't it?"

"Very good."

"I cook well."

"That's sure."

"Even breakfast. I gave it to you in bed. Service of the first class!"

"First class, certainly."

"Then"—a light came on in his eyes—"it won't bother you to pay me a little in advance? Next week's pay this week? That won't bother you? You see, there is my cousin who is sick. . . ."

At their mention, this army of invisible, ever-needful, always devoted-to Algerian cousins I knew it was going to cost me money. Who were they, all these disaster-prone young men—Jeannot didn't seem to have any girl cousins—these young men who not only suffered terrible blows of fortune but who also possessed sterling characters, and yet never had a sou or any access to one except through Jeannot? What fatal star had they all been born under? When would one of them, in good health for a moment at last, make some money of his own?

"Oh, what a shame! Your poor cousin. Which one is it? The one with the glass eye—"

"Not that one. Another one. You don't know this one."

"I don't know any of them."

"That's true," he said thoughtfully.

"The one I would most like to meet is your cousin who had his head operated on."

Jeannot choked on whatever reply he was attempting and, turning squarely toward me, took hold of my arms energetically and glaring at me said: "Are you truly my friend? Are we truly faithful friends? Are we? Eh?"

"Yes, I swear that to you!" For my language was becoming hotter every day, like the food I ate. "That I swear!"

"Well." His face settled into guarded composure. "You know, I do not have all those cousins." He smiled a little at this deception of his. "That is, I have all those and many more, but they are all in Algeria and I am not in contact with them. That money, it was for something else."

"Some of it, I suppose, you have to give to the F.L.N."

Jeannot did not answer that. But his eyes shone for a moment, and I thought I read in them the words, "I am glad you have understood my predicament by yourself."

"I knew you weren't sending that money to any cousins. You take me for an imbecile?"

"You knew!" he cried, full of excited, surprised hilarity; then with a mock frown he gave me a mock punch in the jaw, "You are a deceitful one, you."

"Yes," I said, "yes, I am deceitful."

"Yes," he agreed. "And now, you will let me have a little money?"

I had no money with me, but some more had arrived from Paris and was back at the apartment. I could have told him where the money was—I was fairly sure he already knew, as a matter of fact—and told him how much to take, and I was convinced he would have done just that. I didn't know why I had this conviction. But he would not have agreed to this. He wished me to witness the honesty of the transaction. He had a peculiar reverence for honesty, in the way that people have a reverence for movie queens or miraculous apparitions: because they are so exceedingly rare. Honesty, in Jeannot's life a prize as rarely encountered as water in the Sahara, excited an awed reverence in him.

Now that the money was assured, now that the cousins had been banished, Jeannot turned to other concerns. We walked up the Boulevard of the Sun under palms and roses with cars parked all over the sidewalks, I wearing just a pair of trunks, and Jeannot began repeating his grievances against the police, the war, wages, fate. He sighed, and then added as an afterthought, and a platitude, "I'm going to pay for this unhappiness."

"What?" I said, thinking I had misunderstood.

"I said I'm going to pay, I'm going to suffer because of this unhappiness."

"What do you mean? In the future you will pay for being unhappy now?"

"Yes, of course."

"But you don't *pay* for unhappiness. Do you? You pay for *happiness*. I always thought so."

"No, of course not. How could that be? If you let yourself be unhappy now, then you pay for it in the future. Naturally."

"But why should you? It's not logical. If you're happy now, then you think, Well, some day I'll pay for this, some day there will be the reckoning, some day I'll get the bill."

"No-o-o-o," he said almost in disgust, "it's not like that. Life is different. You are not grown up. You don't understand."

"How do you understand it?"

"There's nothing to understand. It's simple. If you are happy it is as though you plant a garden carefully with good seeds, with lots of water and good weather and attention. Then you get a good crop in the future naturally, isn't that true?"

"Yes."

"But if you are *un*happy, it is as though you are planting a bad piece of earth with inferior seeds and no water. There are plenty of tears, but they are no good. Too salty. So what happens in the future? A bad crop. You are unhappy now and so you reap a bad harvest in the future from what you are doing now. It's all connected, it's natural. If you are unhappy now, it's bad, it's evil. Unhappiness *is* evil, true?"

"True."

"Then how do you expect good to come from evil? It's not possible."

"I see what you mean."

"I am very bad," he said in an almost contrite voice, shaking his head, "very evil, because I allow all this *unhappiness* in my life. And so," he sighed resignedly, "I will suffer for it in the future. If you're happy you will get more of the same, and if you're unhappy you will get more of that."

So happiness reproduced itself and built on itself, and unhappiness did too. I frowned grimly at my own bare feet. "Life is not fair."

"Not what?"

"Fair."

He didn't answer. Fair: the word didn't have any meaning for him. His life had never after all been fair. To expect that was like expecting to live forever or to change overnight into General de Gaulle.

Many people were passing us on the streets: young people in briefest bathing suits—French; long young men in hanging white shirts and knee-length white shorts that looked as though they were boiled daily—English; square young men in flapping pants and miasma sports shirts—American; intermediate-sized youths in dark and shabby clothes—Algerian. The women, more adaptable, all began, whatever their origin, to look French as quickly as possible.

An Algerian came toward us, rather tall for an Arab, with long shiny black hair and black eyes, a dark aquiline face, broad shoulders, better dressed than other Arabs in a closely tailored striped gray suit. Then I noticed with surprise that he was the one Jeannot had been arguing with in the bar that night: with surprise because they were clearly not going to acknowledge each other. Had I not seen them together, the only way I might have detected that they were acquainted was in the definite way they did not look at each other, and in a fleeting rigidity there seemed to be in both their bodies for an instant, a curt quick mutual recognition and rejection.

"Who was that?"

"That?" he said calmly. "I don't know."

"I thought you did."

"No."

We reached the apartment and I gave him a week's pay, 10,000 francs, about $24 at that time officially.

Jeannot took the money and went out. After he left, I started to think about him. What was he really like as a person? But here by the Mediterranean answers did not come so directly as they did elsewhere; perhaps that was why few people here asked direct questions. I could not answer mine, but I did have intimations of the answer, traces of feeling and edges of emotion like the rings of a target in which the bull's-eye is missing: Jeannot cheerfully taking the rag out of my hand to wash my car for me; singing those songs in that attic alone; his assertive penniless pride before the police of a country not his own; and those birds, those little birds that needed those crumbs . . . and his manner, stealthy but with a certain hardy grace, of easing his way into my apartment and my life. He reminded me in that of a dog—I couldn't help it—I had once who loved to lie on the couch, which was forbidden. He would wait until I was safely preoccupied and then he would stand for a while with his forelegs on the couch, watching me carefully. Knowing a leap up would be fatal, he would then slowly raise one hind leg, and after getting that paw on top of the couch he would then draw the rest of himself slowly and a little guiltily but nevertheless willfully up onto the cushions. Such care and guile forced me to let him stay there for the evening. What affected me was, I think, his fortitude, in a world commanded by figures so much more powerful than he was, struggling so gamely to cope with them, to lead his life somehow among all these curt, powerful forces—the way Jeannot did.

||||||||||||||||||||||

Juan-les-Pins was all bamboo and sun, all cha-cha-cha and nakedness and cars. But since people had lived here for so long, no town on the coast could succeed in being entirely frivolous, all surface, even when it tried as hard as this one. There was always a long echo to be heard everywhere, an echo with a certain dignity if only because it came rolling down from so long ago. The echo at Juan-les-Pins, incongruously enough, happened to be the longest and most crucial in all France.

It is to be found in a park near the casino, in the form of a little arch that was made from a trophy shattered and stuck together again. The trophy commemorated the first victory of the Romans in Gaul, which took place on a nearby plain, in 154 B.C. Shattered and stuck together again, war; shattered and stuck together again, war. It was the history of France.

Back on the beach, that afternoon, as France continued to come apart around us, I entered the restless hour by the side of Mireille. She could not be thought of as a substitute for Liliane, but at least she had seen her, at least she could talk about her. As she talked a little nervously in the long steady sunshine of late afternoon, the immobile hour when life stands still and anxiety begins to move, she and I understood several things about each other without mentioning them. Mireille realized that I couldn't think or talk about much except Lili that afternoon and that if she wanted me to stay

111

with her she would have to do that. I saw that she realized this and had accepted the terms. But you were expected to pay for an accommodating conversationalist at Juan-les-Pins in some coin or other, and at the climax of the nervous hour she said: "Will you go with me to the Black Hat tonight? They are going to choose the handsomest Apollo."

"You want to look at all the male bodies?" This was also the frank, or rude, hour at Juan-les-Pins.

She looked at me blankly. "Yes."

"All right."

"I'll meet you at ten."

"All right."

At nine in my apartment, after a bath in the sit-down tub that gave just enough hot water to reach my knees and then turned cold, I was dressing—chino pants, sandals, a loose blue sweater—for a formal Juan-les-Pins evening, and so was Jeannot, in shapely blue-black double-breasted suit, white shirt, calm necktie, cuff links, pointed black shoes. "Where are you going? To a funeral?"

"No," he said quietly, "I'm going out with a girl, a woman. We're going to a night club."

"So am I. So are we."

"Dressed like that! You're crazy, no?"

"Everybody dresses like this in the evening here."

"Me, no," he said flatly. He was carefully working over his thick hair in front of the mirror. He turned, and I suddenly saw not a Mediterranean boy, a car washer and tray carrier, but a young Arabian noble, an heir to the great empire and to the scholars of Egypt. He saw that I admired his appearance, and smiled widely, which made him look like a boy again, and then, turning for the final orientation of his necktie, he was again this young noble from the great and ancient civilization. I began to feel almost fly-by-night.

"No one who has lived in America knows how to dress properly," he said matter-of-factly.

"No? But this is the way the people here dress."

"Still, it's American, improved, but still American. The best here continued to dress as I do. Classic. What you have on, that's fantasy, no good."

He went out, leaving just a trace of dark male perfume behind.

I stood indecisively for a minute, and then I thought: Well, he has to dress carefully or they wouldn't let him in. I can wear anything I want. I didn't admire this thought in myself; it took its place beside my mean remark to Mireille as the two blows I had struck this particular day because of Liliane. I had been unhappy. I was still unhappy. And I was paying for it.

At the door of the Black Hat I found Mireille amid the blaring music wearing the latest thing; a skin-tight purple leotard, made out of flannel perhaps, which had a circular neck and came down her arms to just below the elbows and down her legs to the knees. Over that she wore a crinkly thick gold-and-purple skirt slit in front to the waist. Her teetery-heeled shoes were made of something that looked like glass. Her nails were purple and so was her lipstick. There were two tiny purple lines flaring from the ends of her eyes. She was so tanned that she was darker than Jeannot. Her black hair was set in a straight rigid wave going up and away from her face, and down and under in a smooth unrelieved surface of hair. Her earrings were large, dangling, and purple. "You're in grand toilette," I said.

"Did you have to wear that blue sweater? I'm in purple."

"Yes. You are."

"Everybody knows you have blue eyes. You don't have to dramatize them constantly."

"I must use whatever advantages I have, to hold you."

"Not very good at that," she said vaguely, "holding women, I notice." Then turning back to look at me, "Do you have enough money?"

"I think I do."

"I brought some, in case you can't pay the bill," she said. "Most boys in Juan-les-Pins can't, I find."

"All right."

"You're supposed to be so rich. You at least would have enough, I thought."

"I don't want to spend it all—"

"On me?"

"What I meant—"

"I know what you meant. Come on."

Inside the Black Hat it was very dark and crowded, with latticework and potted plants here and there, a few alcoves and many tiny tables. The small dance floor alone was bright, unnaturally, glaringly bright amid the encompassing murk. The show had already begun, and the master of ceremonies was making a number of jokes about his being Jewish.

"I hate Jews when they're self-conscious about it," said Mireille as we sat down. Then looking swiftly at me, "You aren't Jewish, are you?"

"No."

"I didn't want to insult you."

"I wouldn't consider it an insult."

"Oh, I see, yes. Enlightened."

"You're absolutely entrancing tonight."

"No, admit it. You really don't like Jews, not really, do you?"

"Don't be silly, Mireille."

She gazed at me steadily and then emitted a sound like a neutral grumble.

We ordered the only beverage available at the Black Hat—Scotch, at $1.50 a shot. There was no reason for limiting service to this particular drink unless it was that the Scotch was not native in France, expensive to import, and wrong for the climate. Mireille forced it down, said, "That does me good," with watering eyes, and asked for another.

The comedian went away.

The music at the Black Hat was stereophonic and came through a screen that filled the far end of the room. It engulfed us, seeming to come not only from the far end of the room in a wall of sound but flooding out from under the table as well and raining down from the ceiling. An instrumentalist with bells seemed to be standing just behind my ear. This tide of sound and her second Scotch were exhilarating Mireille; her eyes darted, her earrings swung, and then through the music her voice penetrated to me. "Oh, the Jews, the Jews!"

"Still on that?"

"Oh, I'm so glad you came with me tonight," she suddenly said with unexpected intensity. "So glad. What a relief! I can't tell you. You see," more Scotch, "I've been having a little romance, and now it's finished, last night, last night finished it. It started the night before, so you see it really was a little *little* romance. Tiny." She drew a sharp breath. "But it was sweet, you know, short but sweet, very, very short and sweet. I was silly about it; I can't control myself always; I'm terribly emotional sometimes. Well, then, that's what happened; my emotions ran away with me once, and that started it, and then they ran away with me again, and that finished it. So I suppose I can't really blame them, can I? I owe all the sweetness to them, don't I?"

"Who was it? Do I know him?"

"No, I don't suppose so. He passed quickly through here with the latest tidal wave. Just a boy, a student from Paris. Black hair. A dreamy expression on his face. He was really someone quite *sweet;* he had a vulnerable quality that—well, you know, I'm one of those —when I meet someone vulnerable, and sweet—" She took a deep breath, stopping just short of crying. "Do you know what happened?" nodding at me, with a fixed, birdlike look in her eye, "He turned out to be Jewish."

"I don't understand this obsession you have about the Jews. What have they ever done to you?"

"He turned out to be Jewish, last night. There we were, in my apartment—it wasn't last night; it was this morning; I didn't throw him out in the dark. He was talking about some foolish old man, and he used a Hebrew word to describe him. I don't," she went on quickly, "know any Hebrew words but I recognize the sound, and so I just said quickly: 'Get out. You're Jewish, aren't you? Get out now, please.' I can't help it. I can't *stand* Jews! And to think I had made love to him! I can't tell you how that made me feel! I can't tell you!"

"Mireille," I broke in, suddenly feeling something surprising about this story, "you aren't Jewish yourself, are you? That isn't it, is it?"

She looked at me quaveringly, suspended like a vase trembling on the edge of a table, and then she began to cry, clutching her face with her hands. I tried to say something, ordered another Scotch instead, and, looking uncomfortably around, I noticed Jeannot across the room at a table. He's an Arab, I reflected in this new context of Jewishness, so he and Mireille are enemies. The rest are French, and he and they are enemies too.

The music flooded among us all as we sat looking happy and candid, young people out for the evening, nothing more serious in view than who danced the best cha-cha-cha and who was going to pay the bill.

Jeannot got up to dance. His partner was a rather tall girl in a print dress. She looked as though books meant more to her than life did. On first thought she seemed the last type of girl Jeannot would take out; on second thought she seemed what he would want. She was respectable; he was an Arab in France. I noticed speculative glances at them from others on the dance floor, French couples, glances that were not exactly disapproving—that attitude would have been grotesque at Juan-les-Pins—but unsympathetically analytical. These other French looked at the European girl dancing with Jeannot as though the dress she had on was a curious example of bad taste, that was all.

Jeannot could not really dance. He maneuvered cheerfully around the floor, though, picking his feet up and putting them down with the music while the girl smiled pleasantly and tried to follow. He had a look of pleased adventureness on his face, as though this was an experiment he thought would fail but was happy to try.

When the music ceased, like a waterfall being turned off, they

116

came past our table and he introduced the girl to me. I then introduced both of them to Mireille. It was the most formal exchange I had ever seen at Juan-les-Pins. Jeannot had wanted it that way.

I asked them to sit down with us for a minute, and he accepted without a trace of awkwardness even though he would not come near me on the beach. There was some sphinx-like distinction there which I could not make out.

Four more Scotches were brought. The two girls and I tasted ours. Jeannot attempted his cautiously, grimaced, remarked, "Undrinkable stuff, isn't it!" and put his glass aside. "I long for a little red," he added nostalgically.

Mireille was by now very dry-eyed, and very dry-spirited too, wrung out and dried up and nervous. "You have enough to pay for these, I hope," she said to me.

"I can—"

But Jeannot, nonplused, broke in: "But of course he has! And I too, I must offer you a drink. We must have four more. Where is that waiter?"

"Very gentleman," Mireille murmured in English to me.

Jeannot's eyes flashed quickly to her, then to me.

"Yes," I answered in French, "he's a good comrade."

"Yes," she said dryly.

Jeannot began talking to the girl with him, a European of mixed background from Oran. Gradually it dawned on me that he was speaking Spanish to her, easy, fluent, unthinking Spanish. I couldn't understand a word; neither could Mireille. "I didn't know you spoke that," I cut in.

"Yes," shrugging slightly.

"What else do you speak?"

"Well, Arabic of course, and Italian."

"French," I said, "Spanish, Italian, and Arabic."

"These Mediterraneans," Mireille sighed in English.

"And what languages do you speak, Mademoiselle?" he asked.

"French," she said with an air implying that French and speech were identical. "Ah, yes, and also English."

"Badly," I said.

She glanced distastefully at me and then returned to her drink.

The music gushed out again and we all got up to dance, Jeannot and his girl making their way perseveringly around the floor, and Mireille and I quickly losing contact with each other. For the music was a mambo, and it developed that Mireille had many intricate variations to do, that she was basically a soloist. She was quick and agile and pulsating, every joint of her body rhythmically at work, the long purple earrings flailing against her cheeks, segments of her unrelieved sweep of hair beginning to separate.

"Enough," I said as she pulsated past me. "Enough. Come here." She allowed herself to join me, but to dance close to her was impossible, because of her knees moving rapidly in and out, banging against mine, and her elbows and shoulders uncontainably vibrating.

Finally I persuaded her to leave the floor; as we did so Jeannot waved us to his table. It was necessary for him to buy us that drink. As we sat down an older couple stopped to chat with Jeannot's girl. Then they sat down too. We were all six wedged together around the tiny table. Jeannot would insist on paying for it all, of course. I hoped he had enough money with him. The older man, clipped and pink-faced and white-haired, began talking immediately to Jeannot with surprising intimacy and ease, considering that they had just met and that Jeannot was clearly an Arab and the man seemed clearly to be an upholstered bourgeois of the solidest sort, in the Black Hat tonight because his wife had wanted to look just once into a den of the Rats of the Riviera, the disorderly post-postwar youth she's been reading about in the picture magazines. The man continued talking in his close, confiding fashion with Jeannot. Could it be, was it possible that he was a gay veteran homosexual after all, and his "wife" really his Lesbian sister? Or were they married but penniless, cadging drinks from anyone and everyone? I tried to understand what was going on, using the terms of reference I'd learned on the Riviera.

Jeannot responded to this steady, affable stream of attention, the fluent friendliness, the back slap, the arm squeeze, the arch glance, with a look of cautious pleasure; he was very polite and very responsive but he was also holding himself in check; there was a reservation somewhere in his attitude, although he kept smiling, insincerely, at him. I was dimly surprised to notice this: insincerity seemed so incongruous on the face of Jeannot.

The music ceased and the man's voice carried to me across the table—"good workers, always loyal and reliable, I found, if one treated them well. That's all, good treatment, and then one was repaid with their best side. You expect that from us, don't you?"

"Yes, undoubtedly."

"You expect that from us and you receive it, except perhaps from certain badly reared people. I know you, I know you people there very well. Fine people, brave! My best years were spent there, I tell you frankly, my best years! Not in Paris, not in France. No. There!"

"My best years too," Jeannot said, "were spent there."

"Of course," the man agreed automatically.

"Let's go back to our table," said Mireille, who wasn't listening. She got up, not speaking to anybody. Jeannot rose to recognize that a lady was leaving the table. I thanked him for the drinks.

Back at our table she said: "A bourgeois and an Arab. Name of God, the company you find on the Riviera! What a gay evening in Bohemian, mad Juan-les-Pins! A fat bourgeois and an ignorant Arab. We can do better than *that*, all the same."

The master of ceremonies came out again, the music began again, somewhat more softly, playing *My Man,* and the Contest for the Handsomest Apollo of the Riviera began. They came out one by one in minute trunks—red, green, blue, black—and advancing into the sharply defined circular arena of light, which was shot with drifting cigarette smoke, each raised a mighty arm to reveal a swelling chest, hard belly, and the curving muscles of their legs. The male body had caught the Riviera's attention this summer, either in women's clothes or in next to no clothes. I recognized the third contestant, an Indian-chief-faced massive Arab with immobile features and dancing black eyes whom Jeannot had told me about. He was a marijuana-smoking dishwasher. Tonight he was trying to rise from the dishwashing to the marijuana-dreaming, and we applauded; he seemed impressive and significant under the theatrical lights, backed by the lacing music, the whole smoky charged atmosphere of the Black Hat. The dirty dishes had been left behind in the sink, the marijuana after all discarded because this was going to be real; and it was real for almost a minute as his magnificent muscles rolled in front of us and he reached up toward the heights of the Côte d'Azur, the world of the great cars and walled villas, the layer where the extra life was, where all the big things were, where whatever you had in you came out in its significance. Then he lowered the rolling arm, turned his Indian head on its pedestal neck, and walked barefoot out of the light.

The next Apollo I recognized with a start: Max. Max glistening with oil from his sweep of yellow hair to his planted naked feet, Max in a little red strip of trunks; the applause rolled up for him, and I saw his face turning slowly and solidly red and I was able to read his mind: there was no thought anywhere in it; his mind was like a blood vessel suddenly and completely blocked with a clot, all thought and all sensation stopped by a hard clot of consternation that did after all formulate itself into a single concept: It is impossible that I am in this room. His motor functions remained working; he struck the three or four exhibitionistic poses, he turned in several directions, and the audience applauded enthusiastically; his physique was not so close to perfect as some of the others, but the applause was for his face. At last he was able to walk off.

"Something is lacking in Max," said Mireille, frowning.

"He's younger than the others, and so—"

"I don't mean that."

Then they came out again one by one for a bow, with the winner to be decided by the applause. The Arab finished first, Max second.

I paid the large bill, with a little help from Mireille, and we walked away, she complaining about having had to contribute.

Suddenly changing the subject she said, "You won't talk about our conversation tonight, will you?"

"No."

"You will, of course, but I don't want you to."

"No, I won't."

"You will, you will. But in any case, who cares? One little affair, who could care? So I don't see why you would *bother* to discuss it."

"I'm not going to."

"Who would be interested? And then—and then you have your details so wrong. Imagining that I was Jewish . . ."

"I'm out of money and I'm tired tonight. I think I'll go home."

"Will you? Well, it was fun; the dancing was, at least. Not your unpleasant friends. Where do you find them? I'm not going home." She started back toward the heart of Juan-les-Pins. "I'm going—"

"Yes, have a good time."

"Yes, perhaps. One never knows."

"No. There are still a lot of people out."

"Yes, well, good night."

"Good night, Mireille."

"Remember," trying for a smile, "you're not going to talk!"

"I told you I wouldn't."

"You will, everyone does, but *don't!*"

"All right."

"There must be someone attractive to be found. If I go down to Pam-Pam."

"Probably."

"Well, then, you silly old gossip, good *night.*"

"Good night, Mireille."

I went into my building, stepped through the blackness into the elevator, and began to grope for the light. Then I heard Jeannot's voice coming down the shaft from the floor above; he was saying good night to the girl, who must live in this building. I had never seen her going in or out; leave it to Jeannot to meet her and say nothing about it. He was not showing off any more; they were talking in French.

". . . if you would be able to go out again soon," he was saying.

"That would please me very much. I thank you again for such a nice evening. The dancing—"

"My dancing is the worst, *the* worst," he said with a low giggle.

"Why, no—"

"Oh, yes. But all the same it was a great pleasure for me, dancing with you, because you have grace. You have it."

"That's nice," she said, "very nice."

"It is easy to be nice to you, because you yourself are nice. Certain ones are not, to us Algerians."

"All that is silly."

"Isn't it! Isn't it!"

"Very silly."

A short silence, Jeannot surely glowing that this European girl —so plain and respectable—thought that all that was silly. Visions of respectability must be dancing in his head. And so he said good night, kissed her, I guessed—it might well have been on the hand, and after that gently and shortly on the lips—I respect you, I desire you, in that order—and then her door closed, and while I stood mulling silently in the dark Jeannot pushed the elevator button on his floor and I was suddenly whisked up face to face with him.

"You!" he said, frowning, "What are you doing there hiding?"

"Who's hiding? I'm en route to my place, as you see. Get in."

"She is nice, very nice, don't you find?"

"Yes, she certainly is."

And that Mireille, is she nice?"

"Mireille is complex."

"Yes," he said less enthusiastically, "she has the air."

"Very complex."

"Jewish, no?"

"I don't know, why?"

"One needs to know." We were passing the silent and empty floors one by one, and a line of windows behind the elevator shaft cast segments of pale light at intervals on his calm face. "Me, I pretended to be a Spaniard once, you remember?" He slapped his leg at the ridiculousness of it. "But this girl, I told her right away: 'I am Algerian,' I said, and she said, 'I am half French and half Spanish.' And a little later I said, 'Would you like to go and dance some night?' and she said, 'Yes, I would like that very much,' and there you have why tonight was such a pleasure. She went out, you see, with me. It was me. Like that. It's not good to pretend, not good. It makes you . . . sick inside. No?"

"I think you're right. Yes, I think you are."

"Yes," nodding slowly, "it makes you sick inside."

We reached the top floor. Jeannot was very happy tonight. "After you, Monsieur," he said with a formal bow at the door. As I went by him he suddenly kicked me moderately hard.

"Oh, excuse me, Monsieur."

"For what?" I asked, looking surprised.

"Oh, well," he said, "Oh, well, then . . ." and he started to kick me again.

"Sit down, crazy Arab," I pushed him into a chair in the living room. "We are going to have a hat of night."

"A . . . ?"

"Hat of night."

"What is that?"

"It's something they have in America."

"Yes? What's the American word for it?"

"Nightcap."

"Nightcab."

"Nightcap."

"So much the better. It seems to be something to drink. Unless those glasses you're holding are to wear on our heads?"

"Something unusual is going to happen to your head. Try this." I handed him a glass with two shots of an expensive American bourbon.

He thought it was like wine. Before I could say more than "It's necessary to—" the bourbon was tossed down his throat. Jeannot looked extremely surprised for a second, and then opening his mouth and eyes very wide, as though the fire could escape through all three, he began to cough and laugh and exclaim, as several shades passed over his face.

"Good, eh?"

"Everyone to his taste," he said, breathing deeply.

"You must drink it slowly; here, have another shot, and don't drink it suddenly like that. Try to be civilized."

"We invented civilization," he said, his voice still hoarse from the bourbon.

"You!"

"Not polite to point. Try to be civilized, all right? We invented it."

"Do you always—"

"We invented it and taught you how, you other Europeans."

"Do you always dress like that to go out at night?"

"I don't go out very often. When I do, yes, I dress like this. Why do you wear those clown clothes?"

"It's the style. You never tasted bourbon before."

"Never. It is even worse than that other drink, that Scotch. Why do you drink it?"

"It's the style. You can learn to like it, if it's not too much against your religion."

"Ah, religion—" a futile wave of the hand. "God isn't going to take care of you." A conspiratorial wink. "You have to defend yourself in this world."

"That's true."

"Yes," nodding, "you have to defend yourself in this world." He took a gingerly sip of his drink, his eyes rounded, his face with a listening expression, and after slowly swallowing it he looked around, out through the open glass doors, and said: "Those stars are nothing compared with ours. Over there, at home, we have stars as big as oranges. Over there . . . Did you watch me dance tonight?"

"Yes. Sure."

"Good, eh?"

"Very good."

"Like this. It's like this, dancing," and he began to step around the room, elbows and shoulders swinging in rhythm, a concentrating, amused expression on his face, "It's like this."

"But I think that is the greatest solo dance I ever beheld in my life."

A wide grin.

"Have some more bourbon."

"All right. Can you do the belly dance? That's very popular over there, no?"

"A little."

He began to roll the muscles up and down his stomach. "You have to have control. Try."

So I tried.

"No control," he said definitely, "no control at all."

"No, eh?"

"No. Not at all."

"Ah, well—"

"Yes. Listen," said Jeannot, suddenly concentrating, sitting down in front of the open balcony. In the far corner of the room one small yellow lamp burned. The rest of the light filtered vaguely in from the balcony as he sat concentrated in front of it. "Do you want to see something beautiful some day?"

"Of course. I already see something beautiful. Every day. Here, the Riviera is beautiful."

"Oh," an impatient shake of the head, "this, it's nothing. But nothing. At home, ah, that is something . . . unimaginable," his eyes glowing, and his face coming alive with a particular shine reflected from remembered happiness. "At home there are palms like great fans, and the sky is everywhere, all around—you understand?—no matter where you look there is sky, sky, sky," his voice getting husky recalling it, "and the towns are white, *white*," frowning as his voice intensified, "and toward the South, where my father kee—kept his cattle, we would ride, without a saddle, with nothing, we would ride and ride under this great sky full of these stars like oranges at night, and then when we came to a little village—they knew us, for my father was well known, well loved." He hesitated over the beauty and value of this word and this condition: well loved. "We would be received with honor. Those people there, you understand, they had no alcohol, nothing to smoke, they knew nothing about these city things"—and he smiled slightly, shaking his head a little at the innocence of it; "they were very simple, it was very rustic, they were very welcoming." He pondered all that sand and sky and welcome for a moment, and then, cocking his head, looked at me intently and said: "That was my downfall, because when I came here to the Côte d'Azur it reminded me of home, and so I stayed. I would have done better to have gone north, to Paris, to the industrial places. There is the money, there is the success. But it is cold, *cold!* I was there once, for a month. I was *cold!* You can't know how cold it was there. I couldn't stay," firmly, assertively, "I couldn't stay. I came back here, where the weather is at least tolerable most of the time, and the trees, and some smell in the air, you know that smell? like making love?"—I nodded; other people knew that smell, then, and knew what it was saying—"where those things reminded me, a little, of at home. I stayed here. That was my downfall," and then he lowered his head and looked almost shyly at the floor.

"But then why did you stay here? Why didn't you go home?

126

Now, with the war going on, it would be more difficult, but before, why didn't you go home before?"

He looked up, several feelings contending on his face, and then said in a low voice: "You want to know the truth? You are my friend, it is true. I don't go home, I couldn't go home, because I was ashamed." He smiled faintly and blinked once or twice. "When I went away it was to achieve success, to make them proud of me, my parents. I am the first-born, you see. They love me, they love me very much. They waited four years, no child, no child, no child, no child: *Four years,* and then," his hands slowly and naturally rose in a gesture of almost beatific revelation, "and then I was born," he said in a quiet and slightly awed voice. His hands came down on his knees. "They were happy, *happy!* And when I went away it was to make them proud of me. And so, so like this, me, look at me, a miserable, nothing else, I cannot go home like this, I cannot, I am ashamed."

"But then you must have a success!" I exclaimed, with an optimistic flare from the bourbon.

"Yes!" he agreed vigorously. And then very simply, almost trustingly, "but how?"

"Well, well, then—I don't *know.* What can you do? What do you like to do?"

"I like to cook, I am a good chef. And then I like sports. I played football before, and I was a star. Really. Very strong."

"There! You could play on the team at Nice. That must be good work, well paid."

"Perhaps, perhaps," sudden doubt shadowing his face, "but I am not able . . . because . . ."

"What's the matter?"

Brusquely, "If I played for Nice I would make them better."

"So?"

"Well, then, I can't because—we are not supposed to help Nice, or any part of France, at the moment; we are not supposed to build up their prestige in sports or anything else because—"

"Oh. The war."

He suddenly sprang up, the chair under him banging to the floor, and looming in front of the soft Mediterranean night sky he cried excitedly, *"It was their fault!"*

"The French?"

"Yes! It was their fault! The French are barbarians! They are monsters! Vicious! Detestable!"

"Why do you stay here, then?"

"Me, me? I stay here because I work here—"

"You haven't a true job. Why stay in their country if they're so detestable? You say you liked the Riviera—"

"Yes, it was like home, but—"

"You do like it here, in spite of everything."

A short, balancing pause. Then quietly, "Yes." He stared in front of him. "I love France. You know? I loved France, I mean. But," he shrugged, a worldly, a M. Marc, a Parisian shrug, and said in his easy, unaccented French, "they don't like us. They think we're shit. So it's impossible, nothing to be done. They don't like us." He was sitting down again, elbows on knees, hands clenched in front of him, staring ahead. "That monsieur tonight at the café," he went on without bitterness, "did you hear him? He called me *tu*. At my age. I am a 'boy' to him; we are all 'boys' and always will be 'boys' at any age to him. Nice 'boys' sometimes. But always 'boys.'"

"So you're a rebel? You're with the F.L.N.?"

"No," resignedly, "all that is nothing. I don't like politics. I understand nothing about it." He stood up, glared at me, and yet speaking with an oddly calm, resigned air he said, "Only, I understand that the French," shaking his head with grave dignity, "don't value me." It was the most important thing Jeannot ever said to me. Nothing in life was so important to him as being "well loved"; it was a phrase that recurred continually in his conversation. Here was the admission of deepest defeat. It was as though a young American, at the very outset of adulthood, said, "I'm going to be a failure."

"I can gain nothing from this war," he went on. "I only lose, whatever happens."

"That's a sad thought."

"Sad." He shrugged and looked with faint amusement at me because of the pitiful inability of this word to express the nightmare of Algeria and Algerians. "It's fatal, that's all."

After sitting staring for a while he said, "Are you really a Russian?"

"Yes."

"Yes, but are you really a *Russian?*"

"Yes, I am. I haven't turned into an American yet. It takes a long time to turn into an American. Just when you think you've got it, you find you're being *careful* again, about the wrong thing. You have to have a lot of nerve to be as careless as an American. I haven't got that kind of nerve."

"I don't understand that," he said abstractedly.

"And I'm not French either, because I can't be *that* careful." I shrugged. "So I must be a Russian."

"What's it like to be a Russian?"

"Nothing. It's like nothing. I don't think there are any Russians. My father was 'Russian.' But what he really was was something else. He really was descended from some rich peasants who lived in the Caucasus and some very poor nobles from the Ukraine. *He* was middle class. There never was a middle class in Russia before. He thought he was very educated and European, but my mother always said, You Asiatic!" to him when they argued. She meant it. They were just becoming Russians in my father's day, those Ukrainians and Little Russians and Moslems—"

"Moslems!"

"Some 'Russians' were Moslems. You see? They weren't anything yet, in my father's day at least. There was no *Russian*. Except I think in their anger. I have that; that's authentic. My bad temper is strictly Russian. All of us refugees from the Russian Revolution, the middle-class ones anyway, are—that's what we are, refugees.

We're denationalized. I haven't got a nation. I was a Parisian last winter and I'm a Provençal now and next fall I turn into a New Yorker. Via Air France. I turn into a New Yorker on October 15th, at Idlewild Airport."

He shook his head slowly. "I don't understand that. Me, they say I'm French, a French citizen. But you know," he winked sharply at me, "I don't believe it. I know what I am. I'm Algerian."

"You're lucky," I said automatically.

"Lucky," he repeated, looking at me, and broke into harsh laughter.

IIIIIIIIIIIIIIIIIIII

The next morning—exactly like all the others—shining, still, with hot fresh sunshine and a soft clarity in the air—I awoke to the breakfast of coffee with milk and a *croissant* with marmalade that Jeannot set out on the table holding the vase of flowers, in front of the balcony. The sky formed its flawless dome over the sea toward Algeria, and the other sea, of pine boughs below me, stood motionless, screening the morning hubbub below it in the street; in every way another of the golden, suspended, caressing mornings on the Mediterranean had begun.

He handed me the morning newspaper without saying anything or even expressing anything on his face. A photograph of Sergio the waiter, head and shoulders, stared out from Page One. "But this isn't possible!" I exclaimed, glancing quickly through the story. "He robbed his own *parents?*"

"Yes," said Jeannot collectedly, moving across the room, wearing a pair of white shorts. "All the money in the restaurant gone."

"Where did he escape to?" I asked, searching through the block of type that seemed to resist my reading it—phrases like "the desperate youth" and "the suspected smuggler" bouncing out at me.

"To Paris, or perhaps to Italy. He had confederates there."

"But robbing his parents!"

"He needed to escape—it's all there in the story. The police came for him, because of his contraband business. He was getting too ambitious, it seems. So he needed money to get away. Fast." He went toward the kitchen, nodding humorously to himself. "He certainly got away fast. Read the rest of the story":

"The fugitive, getting into his father's car in front of the restaurant on the pretext of procuring a valise, without warning started the motor and precipitated the vehicle at the police agents. These latter adroitly avoided the oncoming car, but two pedestrians, M. Jean-Pierre Lehoux, 48, of Vallauris, ceramicist, and Mlle. Simone Pelloile, 19, of Lille, a vacationing student, were gravely injured by the desperate one's evasion."

It had all happened late in the afternoon yesterday. The huge mass of people at Juan-les-Pins had insulated us from the news, which during any other month we would have heard in half an hour.

"Poor Sergio. He's crazy."

"Not crazy," said Jeannot sternly from the kitchen. "He understands the world. He lost his gamble, that's all. So he pays, and all the others connected with him pay. It's normal." He stood at the kitchen door, a brooding figure almost the color of cedar, and said: "Personally I could not live like that. You noticed how nervous Sergio has been lately? It's enervating; it makes you distracted. But for himself, ambitious like that," he shrugged, "why not contraband? It doesn't hurt anybody."

"Two people in the hospital. An abandoned fiancée. Two rifled parents."

"Ah, that, that was not because of the contraband. That was because of the police."

"But the *police* were because of the *contraband!*"

"Perhaps. Always bad, the police. They offered me a job as a policeman in Algeria before I came here. Because I was a football star. Strong. I tried it for a week. But what they do! They get some poor one, some suspect, and then Baf! Pow!" he pantomimed forcefully, "Bim! Bam! It is *not* pretty. I don't like that thing. I left. Always bad, the police." He turned back into the kitchen. "Continue reading the newspaper," he said over his shoulder, "there is another thing."

Balancing Sergio's flight was another block of excitable headlines: NEAR NICE A GASOLINE STORAGE STATION IS ENTIRELY RAVAGED BY A GIGANTIC FIRE. And scattered through the subheadlines were "F.L.N." and "Terrorist," the increasingly popular word for the Algerian rebels. Members of the F.L.N. had set fire to the station; it was unknown for how many days it would burn; it could not be predicted when the area would be habitable again. The police, the Minister of Interior announced, would "intensify repression against North African terrorism."

"Well, then!" I said loudly.

After a long silence from the kitchen Jeannot said quietly, "Yes."

"A strange summer."

Another quiet "Yes."

The paper crackled as I followed the story to an inside page. "I think life is going to become more difficult here."

A final "Yes," and in a quieter voice, "for us Algerians."

IIIIIIIIIIIIIIIIIIII

That afternoon Jeannot was out; I was in. I was thinking about Liliane, of course, just thinking about her. I believed that if I thought hard enough it would force her, wherever she was, to think about me. Not everyone is in contact with another person in this way, I believed; only people of a certain sensibility are capable of it. I knew this kind of pseudopsychic belief was the Russian coming out in me, the coarse mystical streak of Old Russia, but there it was. I sat by the balcony, thinking hard about Lili.

The overloud sound of the buzzer tore through the apartment. I went to the door and opened it. A tall, aquiline Arab stood there, the one in fact whom Jeannot and I had passed some days earlier on the street, the one whom he'd been arguing with before that in the café. "Is your servant here, Monsieur, please?"

"My servant? You mean Jeannot?"

"Yes, Jeannot, Monsieur, if you please. Is he at home?"

"No, he's gone out."

His black, liquid eyes looked very deeply and very expressionlessly at me. "It is important that I see him, Monsieur."

"Well, he's out. I don't know where he went."

"If you would be kind enough to tell him that Pierre is looking for him." He continued to look at me expressionlessly, unless there was a certain stern expression about his face. "It is urgent."

"Urgent."

"Yes, Monsieur."

"I'll tell him. Where can he find you?"

"He knows where I will be . . . always the same place," he added with an attempt to be engaging, a failure of an attempt, ". . . a little bar. He knows. But as soon as possible, if you understand. It's urgent."

"All right."

"Urgent," he said once more, unquestionably stern, even severe, now, and then, turning, he left.

▐▌▐▌▐▌▐▌▐▌▐▌▐▌

An hour or so later I went out. A new airliner that Air France had just bought was flying along all the boundaries of France that day as an exhibition, and was due to pass here in a half-hour. I decided to go down to the beach and watch. On the steps of the apartment I ran into Max. "I was coming to see you," he said, a certain sternness in his manner, too.

"I'm surprised that you will show your face today, after the way you showed everything else last night."

He blushed very slightly; something overbore his embarrassment. "That was a screw-up, never again." He grabbed my arm.

133

"Listen. That Arab who works for you. His father's been killed. Does he know about it?"

"What?" I said foggily. "What?"

"Does he know about it? They killed him yesterday or the day before in Algeria. The parachutists. Resisting arrest or some baloney like that. The Algerian crowd here got the word today. Bébère, you know, the one who won that contest last night, he told me just now. Look out, eh? This one with you, what's his name?"

"Jeannot," I said.

"He might get very nasty, even a little dangerous when he hears. You know these Arabs. They think their fathers are like God."

"Killed? That old man?"

"The main blunder was that that old man was the chief of his village or something like that, you know, the big wise man with the beard. Very well respected, and so the other people in town didn't like it when the parachutists were taking him away; they started yelling and the women began making that creepy noise Arab women make and somebody threw some rocks and then the shooting started and when it was all over nobody had been very much hurt except the old man, and he was dead."

I didn't say anything.

"I thought I'd better tell you right away, my pot. Otherwise, who knows, when this Jeannot finds out he might be some trouble for you."

I nodded. Finally I said, "Why were they arresting him?"

"That father, you mean? But I told you. He was a big chief of the village, a big chief of the rebellion too, I guess."

"I see."

"On guard, eh? You never know what these crazy Arabs are going to do. Me, I'm tolerant of everybody. But Arabs, after all, you've got to watch out"—with his index finger he pulled down the skin under his right eye—"watch them, all the time."

I didn't go down to the beach to goggle at the big airplane. I noticed it through my apartment window as it wallowed by, grinding the air with its hypercharged propeller motors, its huge rigid wings shading the sand.

I waited for Jeannot. He came in at about six, and while he had the quiet, methodical nervousness that had been gathering in him ever since he had been picked up by the police, it was obvious that he had not been told. He just looked dogged and dispirited and disinclined to talk. I was glad of that, because I myself had never been more disinclined to talk in my life. I wasn't going to say a word; it was not my place, not my duty, not my ordeal. It was not my war.

We went out to dinner. There was only one restaurant where we could eat together in all Antibes-Juan-les-Pins. Every other restaurant that he liked was too raw for me; every other one I liked was too ceremonial for him. We overlapped on just one, called the Restaurant of the Inn of the Square Fort. It was on the other side of the curving harbor from Old Antibes. We drove along the top of the rampart in the evening—it was in fact nearly dark—and came out beside the water. Across its blue-black surface the restaurant was alight domestically. But behind it was an odd brightness in the dark sky, a reddish, unnatural aura. "That light—"

"Yes," he said. "The storage station in Nice. Still burning."

"I didn't know it could be seen all the way from here."

"That can be seen all the way from everywhere."

We were making the circle of the harbor, and just approaching the halfway point. Beyond us there was just a gasoline storage station and then the restaurant.

Something appeared in the headlights. A policeman. Several of them. Motorcycles. Guns.

I then realized that in the very glow of the Nice holocaust I was driving an Algerian at night up to another gasoline storage station.

I stopped the car where they told me, took my hands off the steering wheel, and dropped them disgustedly on my legs. I deserved whatever was going to happen. Jimmy Smoot himself in full confusion would not have done this.

What happened was a quick and not particularly thorough search of us and the car, a very talkative search. Throughout Jeannot kept a level, metallic smile, and it was only the brightness of his eyes that betrayed any strong feeling. His eyes flared around him, but he said nothing.

The police looked at our identification papers; I explained where we were going. Then three of them on motorcycles went along with us to the restaurant. The proprietress assured them that she knew us well, had in particular known Jeannot for a long time; he had even worked for her once. A good worker. Loved France. Now the police changed, became briskly humorous with Jeannot, and rather courtly to me. When they left us, the one who seemed to be in charge said, "Good appetite," and then, with a French look of pleasure or mockery, "gentlemen."

We sat down to dinner outside, under an arbor. The view from there was one of the most notable in the South of France. At night it was not just a striking view; there was an insubstantial aura about it, the cluttered town across the water from us having more or less vanished except for two solidly square towers shot even higher toward the sky by flaring searchlights from below; these two great tubes of brightness climaxed the scattered port lights and piercing town gleams that formed its wavering base. From this base there was visible the seawall of Roman arches advancing toward us, and ending in a little tower with its own clear light. There was also one little beam of light on the water itself, and this was the most random of all; zigzagging on the water, which had the brilliant blackness of some fatal jewel, one great searchlight roamed erratically here and there, on the prow of a motor launch, night-fishing. All else was scintillating and motionless.

"What did that son of a bitch say!" Jeannot demanded urgently and bitterly across the outdoor table as I sat down. "Making filthy jokes!"

The table between us was crowded with little plates holding paté and sardines and radishes and cucumber and anchovies and cold mushrooms.

We ate for several minutes in silence, with no sound except that of the motor launch puttering over the black water, searching for a fish to snatch out of paradise.

"You know why he said that, don't you?" he resumed in a bitter voice. "He thinks you're lowering yourself, eating in public with me."

"No one thinks anything. Forget about it. Eat."

"Forget about it. That's easy for you to say! Monsieur you can go away any time; you, you're not even involved. You're not even French any more. You can go away to America and forget all about this. Me, I am caught. I am here. If not here, then I am in Algeria, among the grenades and machine guns. And the helicopters from America which search for Algerians in the hills like vultures. I cannot forget about it. Just you can, Monsieur."

"If it makes you feel better to attack me," I said edgily, "go on."

"How genteel Monsieur is! Thank you for your indulgence of a poor miserable one like me."

The waitress came and put before us a fish soup that summed up all that was best in the Mediterranean. When she was gone Jeannot said with clenched teeth: "I suppose I am fired for talking to Monsieur like this. Naturally, I expected that."

"If you call me Monsieur once more, I'm going to throw this fish soup at you."

"You," he grumbled, spooning up some, "you're just a rich man. You are free. Nothing binds you."

We were silent for a while. Jeannot's nerves were getting worse steadily. And now . . . I was not going to tell him; it was not going to be me. The other Algerians would do it better. They had probably had a certain practice, in telling each other of death. They would know how to do it. I could not be expected to.

"Jeannot, what do you—what's the news from home?"

"Bad. What do you want? Always bad. And how I used to wait for the letters from over there! It was the climax of every week, better than the football match, better than most of the girls around here, if you want to know the truth. Yes. But now it is always bad news. My father has a bad time in the cattle business. Everything is in disorder. The ranches, the markets, they are all in a mess. Nothing is sold, nothing is bought. I am not sure," he looked at me blankly, "that they always have enough to eat. My mother! My father! I am not sure—can you understand that!—that they always have enough to eat. It is not possible! But that's the way it is." The waitress put a small, tender steak, a *tournedos* with béarnaise sauce, in front of us. "And so," he went on, I—it's very curious—I wish for *no* letters from my family. Never did I expect to feel *that*. But when I get a letter now it makes me sad for a week, for a month. . . . 'My son, one does not have the necessities here just at present. If you could send us just a little money . . .'" His fork in the air, looking out over the brilliant black water of the port, he recalled with an expression on his face of valuable memory and contained grief the essence of the messages that came from Algeria: " 'I know that life is difficult for you there too, but if by chance you have a little put aside . . .' Aside! Me, I have nothing put aside! I have nothing put ahead, either! I am lucky to have a meal in front of me from day to day! Why do they write me like that? What can I do?" His fork was flung brusquely on the table. "Ah! I can't eat! What's the use. Shit. One of these days, I'm going to die."

Then I had to force myself to say something. I worked myself with an effort into a long explanation of what General de Gaulle was going to do as soon as he got permanent control of the government, which would be soon. I said that the plotting officers in the French Army and the parachutists were not going to take over either in Algeria or in France. De Gaulle was already getting them under control. Soon he was going to present the Constitution of a new republic, the Fifth Republic, in a referendum, and after that, when the people of France had voted for it, things would be better. "Yes," I pressed on, seeing the light beginning to glow again in his eyes, and caught myself by the gathering plausibility of my argument, "once General de Gaulle and the Fifth Republic are established, things will go much better. You're going to see. Order will come back to Algeria, perhaps with independence, perhaps in union with France, I don't know; who cares?"

"Who cares?" he echoed immediately.

"And then order will come back to Algeria, and business will revive, and your mother and fa—"

"Yes?" he was following me with growing eagerness.

"And then business will revive in Algeria—and your family will be fine, all right, as before. Everything will be—everything will be—all right."

"This meat, you know, overcooked a little, don't you think? Or rather—"

"No, it seems all right."

"Perhaps. I just thought that that piece there might have been a little overcooked. Perhaps not. A little more wine? Do you always drink Pommard with steak?"

"Pommard? Why—yes, yes."

No, I could not.

Over dessert—a cool sour cream that came rolled in tin foil and was eaten with sugar—Jeannot said with a reflective half-smile: "When we have that peace in Algeria you mentioned, when De Gaulle—we like him there, he was good to the Arabs during the war—well, then, when De Gaulle has calmed the country, I'm going back there, for a visit. Or maybe I will take my father's business from his shoulders; he is getting old now, old. He is, let's see"—he placed his strong hand with its fingers flat thoughtfully against his cheek, his dark eyes rolled cogitatingly up—"he must be sixty-eight years old now. Sixty-eight! That's old, all the same. I never went home much, I told you, because I was not," a quiet, accepting smile slowly came to his face, "a success, I could not make a good presence; they would not be proud of me, I thought. So I thought for a long time. Yes, a *long* time! But now, I'm changing my ideas. Now, I have another thought. Now I don't believe, to tell the truth, that it matters to them very much if I am a success. In fact I believe that it *never* mattered to them. What they wanted, my father and my mother, was for me to stay there and as their first-born—they waited four years for a first-born, I told you that, no? What they wanted was for the first-born to aid my father and finally to take charge of the business. But me, I had to *travel!* I joined the Foreign Legion, at Sidi-bel-Abbès, one time! Yes!" His face contorted with amusement. "It's true! Me, in the Foreign Legion! I didn't tell you that? Yes, I joined, and after twenty-four hours in the Foreign Legion I began to ask myself if I understood what I had done, and there was a friend of my father's there and he said: 'Come here, son of Kouider. What are you doing here?' I told him, and he pointed out a place under the fence and at night he met me there and lifted up the fence and said, 'Go. Go home. Your father is waiting for you. Tell him what has happened.' Yes, twenty-four hours in the Foreign Legion! My father had to pay quite a bit of money to settle that affair. It was droll! Always he wanted me there, with him, in the business, eventually to take the business, his first-born. But, I don't know, I had something in the head that said *travel*. It's necessary to see the world. It is necessary to be free!"

He stirred his small cup of coffee with a small spoon, smiling softly to himself. "But now I have seen the world. Not too pretty, if you want the truth. He looked at me, frowning a little, "not very beautiful. I have seen Paris. That is beautiful, yes, but not kind. I have lived here on the Côte d'Azur for several years. Rich people from all over the world come here, so I have the impression that this is a paradise, this must be one of the greatest places in the world. All right then, I have seen the world, and now you know what? I think I'll go home to my town in Algeria when I can and see what that is like now. I am not ashamed now; I have worked; I have nothing to be ashamed of; I have done the best possible, so I will go home. They will be happy, my father and my mother, happy! And then, as you say, peace is coming back soon to Algeria, just as soon as General de Gaulle—What's the matter?"

"Nothing, nothing at all."

"You're not getting sick again? Is your head bothering you?"

"No, nothing. I guess I'm tired, that's all."

"Let's go back." He stood up energetically. I got up, picking up the bill with one hand and reaching into my pocket with the other, dropped the money getting it out of my pocket, stooped to get it, dropped the bill, picked both up, and then stood still and shut my eyes for a second or two. Jeannot didn't notice. He was going to have to be told. For one thing, I couldn't stand it any longer.

I paid the bill, and as we went out toward my car Jeannot said, "We'll have to pass the police guarding the storage tanks on the way back." He nudged me, and with an arch wink, whispered, "You have the grenade ready, no?"

"Shut up."

"Soon all the grenades will be put away. You're going to see. De Gaulle to power!"

We drove slowly along the harbor and were waved through the police roadblock. It was late; the Old Town of Antibes preserved just a few havens of sociability, all of them cafés. The rest was shuttered and silent, closed in the nighttime Mediterranean stillness, gray-white old houses like crumbling tombstones. Flowers and ivy, on sills and along walls and filling crevices, were all leaf-still, waxen; the narrow streets were pure echo chambers, waiting to reverberate the dropping of a pebble all over town. Some moonlight and a few lamp beams shone colorlessly white in geometrical fragments here and there on walls; here and there a cave-like café spilled out noise and brightness. The only movement was of water, fountains, and troughs flowing on gently through the night.

We reached the Place de Gaulle, where one café only carried on, and then turned off down the Boulevard Wilson to the Gilded Pine. There the elevator was working but the lights were not. We rose up to the top floor in darkness and in whispers, and once inside the apartment we were fumbling for matches or a candle when the lights came on.

Jeannot quickly went to his own little bedroom in back. I went to the balcony and stared at the pierced hood of night over Cap d'Antibes and didn't see it. I pictured instead a small white village in Algeria. I imagined a sixty-eight-year-old man in robes. I visualized the paratroopers, élite troops dressed for combat. I saw the mother and various people around the house. I imagined the word passing over a wall and down an alley and here and there, passing as it can only in Arab towns, like electricity. I imagined the crowd gathering, the swelling noise, the paratroopers not so much menacing as nervous, tremendously outnumbered; they start into the street with the prisoner, the crowd suddenly turns much more volatile, someone throws something, a lot of others throw things, a furious paratrooper turns to fire, perhaps only fire over their heads; he fires, the old man moves in front of him just at that moment. He's dead in the street.

But was he? That thought broke over me like a dawn. Was he? Were rumors ever more unreliable than in a war? Max might be all wrong. But then I remembered the other one, Pierre, and night swiftly descended again. He had wanted to see Jeannot "urgently." He had the official news. But I was not sure of that and I immediately recognized that I could not speak to Jeannot unless I first made certain with Pierre. Pierre's urgent news might, if Allah willed it, concern something else.

I knew I couldn't sleep, and I decided to go and look for Pierre. There were only a few cafés where he could be, if he was out tonight. I moved silently toward the back hall. Jeannot's door was ajar. I could see him lying on his side, his knees bent as though he were riding a bicycle. There was no sound. He not only never snored; he never audibly breathed in his sleep. At night in his room there was always a complete, suspended, waiting Arab silence.

I stepped quietly out of the apartment, and knowing that the elevator always made a sort of belching noise when it was started I walked down the six flights and out into the vaguely rhythmic sounds of the leftover revels still coming from the center of Juan-les-Pins.

Pierre, as he called himself, would not be there. Very lucky, Pierre, that you have such simple tastes, lucky for me; I don't have to waste time and money at Maxim's and the Old Dovecote and the other stylish cabarets looking for you. For you will not be there, Pierre.

In French, let's see, Pierre would rhyme with "la mer" and "Bébère" and "parterre. . . ." I was walking with my doom-sounding footfalls along the empty streets away from the center of town, into the back streets, darker and darker, toward the railroad station, toward the National Highway, back there where in the poor cafés the Arabs gathered when their work for the day was at last over, and where, as Jeannot once put it, "each one recounts his misery."

There, that rhymed: "misère." Pierre Misère.

That was an evil omen, but there was nothing I could do about it; I could not think of a good word that rhymed with Pierre, not one.

I hoped he might be drunk, hoped he had a typically light Arab head. Then he might tell me the truth. Otherwise he could easily just lie steadily. I couldn't blame him. Who was telling the truth to anybody in this country these days?

Two blank and nearly empty cafés on the left; Pierre was not there.

At the top of the street I came to the railroad station. To the left of it two cafés faced each other on opposite sides of a street, both of them very much frequented by the Arab proletariat of Juan-les-Pins. One café was enclosed and quiet, for talking; the other was open, blazing, with a wild jukebox, and was for shouting, getting drunk, and arguing. Out of this one a crooner's voice pleaded up and down the street:

> *Give me, please, I beg you, give me*
> *A bit of hope, a bit of life, a bit of love. . . .*

No one listened; twenty young workmen were boisterously shouting, getting drunk, and arguing over and through the music.

A young Arab appeared without warning at my left elbow. "You're looking for someone?"

"Pierre . . ."

"Pierre? Tall? Well built?"

"Yes."

"Works at the Hotel Beautiful Shores."

"I don't know."

"It must be the same. He's just over there, past the station, around the corner. You know that café?"

"Yes. Opposite the railroad foot crossing."

"That's it. You have something for a drink? You have a cigarette?"

I handed him some cigarettes and plunged across the small and empty square in front of the silent, dimly lighted little railroad station, the square with nothing in it except the subtle, choking night air of Juan-les-Pins, heavy with ancient durable desires, ways of sexual love, cynicism from the earth itself, a steady, glowing offering of foreordained fulfillment and disillusionment in sexual love.

Turning left just beyond the station, I mounted a short little lane and there, on the right at a bend in the road, was the tiny café, dim and quiet.

Through the curtains I saw two men standing at the bar, and a woman behind the counter. One of the men was Pierre.

Never hesitate; this was a rule of conduct I'd discovered on the Riviera. It won't be understood here. Act. Always and at once, act.

I walked into the dim little room and said, "Good evening, sirs-lady," in the usual formula. All three vaguely replied. Pierre turned slightly toward me, and we nodded. After a silence he said, "Your servant is back, Monsieur?"

"Jeannot is back, yes. If your message for him is urgent—"

"Ah, well, it can wait," adding into his glass, "Nothing to be done about it."

"Let me offer you a drink."

A second's proud pause, and then in a downright voice he said, "And my companion?"

"Of course, and Madame."

"No, thank you, Monsieur." Black-haired, middle-aged, imme-

144

morially self-contained, Madame did not drink in these particular circumstances. Her few words communicated the information that she was the proprietress, she would fill our glasses, she would not be involved. Madame would go on serving the French, serving the tourists, serving the Arabs, serving the devil himself if he had fifty francs. She seemed partly avaricious, partly very civilized, and all French. After serving us, she went into a back room.

"Beautiful weather," I said.

"Always," said Pierre.

"I suppose it will go on for some time."

"Without doubt."

"It doesn't change."

"Never." He took a gulp of the cognac. "Of course, there is the mistral from time to time."

"Yes, there's that. Bothersome, isn't it?"

"Very bothersome."

"It agitates people."

"Evidently."

"There's always something to agitate people."

"Ah—what do you want?—it's like that, life."

"Yes, but here trouble is stranger than other places, because this is a beautiful place here, and it's like—like—"

"Like drowning in a glass of water," he supplied.

"Well, now, I don't know, not exactly."

"It's all the same. Nothing to be done."

"You can do some things."

"About the weather!"

"About trouble."

"Ha. You are a stranger, I think. Here there is nothing to be done. About trouble."

"The two sides can make peace," I said.

"Peace, peace? What are you talking about? Some war?"

"The Algerian trouble, in Algeria and here. The killings here, the bombs, those things."

"That. That will go on until one side wins or the other side wins."

"The sooner, the better."

"The sooner, the better."

"Especially now that civilians are getting involved, old people —Jeannot's father . . ."

"Ah,". he said dully.

"To—to execute a man of that age," I said in a voice as carefully level as possible.

"Not execute! *Execute!* Stupid idea! They shot him at his own house!"

I stared at my cognac, and then said, "That's not possible."

"Before his own family! Like that! Baf! Dead!"

"It's not possible."

"And you think the trouble will stop."

I took a long breath, and tossed some more cognac into my mouth. "Why was he so easy to trap? I thought the men of the F.L.N. were cleverer than that."

"How? What? What F.L.N.?"

"The F.L.N. The rebels."

"Jeannot's father was not of the F.L.N. That's known by everybody."

"Yes, of course, but what I meant—"

"The F.L.N. forced him to give them money, yes. With a machine gun. Then the French found out. They came. That was when they were going to put him in detention, setting an example, because of his importance in the village. Then there was some so-called confusion at his house. Then," he looked at nothing expressionlessly, "dead."

I walked slowly away from the bar and stood near the door.

"How is Jeannot taking it?" he asked quietly.

"Jeannot? He—Jeannot hasn't been told yet."

"Oh," he said in a low voice. Then he went on: "He told me he esteems you very much. He says you are not his boss; you are more his friend. That's what he told me. So I want you to do something for me, for him. He and I have had some arguments. We are friends, but we are not good friends, not exactly. His brother wrote to me to tell him. I have the letter here. Here it is. Take it. You tell him. He will be able to accept it better that way."

I recognized the handwriting on the envelope; it was Jeannot's brother's, his writing brother, the one who corresponded with him on behalf of the family. He wrote in French, but with curlicues and little flourishes and adornments attached to the words that made them look half in Arabic.

Pierre came over to the door. "Jeannot has been neutral; he doesn't like politics," he said; "he ignores all that. They have to force him to contribute to the F.L.N. here. But if I was Jeannot, I would not have to be forced now. And you?"

||||||||||||||||||||

At the apartment I came in quietly and saw that he was still asleep. I had an odd impulse to wake him up and blurt, spill out the whole horror now, in the dead of night, tell the black tale now, in the blackness. Not in the morning, not in the fresh, still, shining morning we were guaranteed by the will of God to have tomorrow, not then; it would be a searing blot thrown in the face of such a morning. But I got into bed and finally, in exhaustion, to the last pulsation of the cha-cha-cha coming from the last night club, I fell asleep.

||||||||||||||||||||

The next morning—there it was, as ever, spread above us—I was sitting at the table and Jeannot was serving me breakfast. He handed me *Nice Matin* as usual, and as usual there was a sensation on Page One. General de Gaulle, it turned out, had presented the Constitution of his proposed Fifth Republic the day before in the Place de la Republique in Paris. No disorders. The F.L.N. was also in the news; it announced that it was going to ruin the economy of France during the next four weeks, through terrorism. I tried to read all this but couldn't keep my eyes or mind on any subject. "What's the matter with you?" Jeannot said. "You are not a target for the F.L.N. Relax."

"Jeannot—"

"Yes."

"Jeannot, I—"

"You what?"

I put my elbows on the table and sank my head into my hands. "I have something I have to tell you."

"What is that? You have an odd air this morning."

"I have something I have to tell you."

Suddenly he came and faced me. "I know. My job. Finished, eh? That's it. I have not worked enough to please you—"

"No, no, no. Forget that."

Relief flooded through him. "Oh, well, then," he headed back into the kitchen. "What is it? Oh. I know. Your wife. She has returned!"

I sighed heavily. "No, it's not that."

"What is this game you play? What is it you want to tell me?"

"Jeannot, it's that—" The Mediterranean had undermined my control without my knowing it; sitting there, trying to speak, my nerves suddenly seemed to give away. "Jeannot, it's your father," I cried out. "He's dead! The French shot him. . . . Pierre told me. . . . He's dead!"

"Oh, no," he said with one of his curving, gentle smiles, coming to the table, holding a dishtowel. "What are you saying?" he asked. "What's troubling you, Nick?"

"It's your *father*," I drove on bitterly; "there was a fight at your house. . . . Some French soldiers were there because he gave to the F.L.N. . . . Something happened. . . . He was shot. . . ."

"No, no, no," he continued in a gentle voice, going back into the kitchen to dry another cup, "it's not possible; you are sick, you have some hysteria this morning—still sick from the other time. Your nerves, bad, eh?" He came back, offering me more coffee and milk. "There, come on, drink. Be calm. You've been overdoing, you're exhausted. You had a nightmare, that was it?" He nodded slightly, his face set with concern. Then he jerked his head sideways, curtly indicating the Antibes police, "It's those sons of bitches stopping us in the dark last night."

"You've got to believe me—what I would give if you didn't—you've got to believe me. . . ."

Jeannot stopped in front of me and lifted up my chin with his hand, looking at me with an expression of concern. "What is it?" he asked quietly.

I saw that I was going to reach him. It was a horrible realization. But looking at him I made my eyes and my face look as collected as possible, and I said in a quiet tone, "I have to tell you that your well-loved father is dead."

The personality dropped from his face and it became a boy's, where anything could happen. "You say that—" he started in a cracking voice, his black eyes, black now, looking excitedly around.

"Pierre told me. Here's a letter from your brother." He stared at it with absolute blankness and awe, as though it were a diamond or a bomb or a plague.

"You say that my *father*—" Then his face broke and he was crying uncontrollably. "You say that my father is *dead!* Dead! You say that!" his voice rising wildly. Then abruptly deeper: "Who do I kill? Who? Tell me who has done it!" He grabbed the front of my shirt, dragging me out of the chair, "Tell me who I must kill!" He hit me glancingly on the face, to punish the place from which this news had come, tears streaming from his tightly contorted face, "Tell me, *tell* me!"

I buried his head against me, and he grabbed me, his fingers digging into my back until I fought myself free before I began to bleed, "I will kill them," he croaked, "I will kill them, I will kill them."

"There is no one to kill," I said. "It was the French Army."

"I will kill them!" He plunged across the room and drove his fist through the glass door, "and then I will die! You see! Bleeding,

149

bleeding! Blood! You see! It's that! That's it, that's what there will be! On the earth where my father was killed there will be blood, all, all blood! *Their* blood! I will make *blood* to drown my father's blood! You will see! May God," he said in a lower, trembling voice, "take out my eyes, I will avenge the murder of my father. You," he said in a stranger's voice to me, "are my witness."

IIIIIIIIIIIIIIIIII

That night he disappeared. He took everything that belonged to him out of the apartment when I was not there, scrupulously remembering his possessions down to which scrap of underwear belonged to him and which to me.

It was September. The crowds were dwindling quickly away. Losing yourself at Juan-les-Pins and losing contact with those you knew became more difficult every day. Yet Jeannot simply ceased to exist; he was nowhere.

I did not know what to do.

And so, with the perverse streak that determined me to come to the holocaust of the Riviera in the summer to get over damaged nerves, I took up underseas diving to escape from my problems and Lili's and Jeannot's and France's. Underseas diving I knew to be a nerve-racking sport; that's why I chose it. I had never understood people who sought "peace and quiet." I looked for peace in the middle of a howling hurricane of action, in the silent eye at the center.

That month the hurricane howled with a higher, a banshee shriek through France. I discovered the rising note every morning, over coffee, in *Nice Matin*. Paris had collapsed into a vaudeville nightmare, a slapstick tragedy: Italians and Portuguese who happened to be living there were being accosted by the jumpy police, who took them for Algerians and took all Algerians for terrorists; the Italians and Portuguese, not good at the French language and fearful by definition of the police, often panicked and ran, pursued by wildly shooting police. A pleasant steamer that had made the crossing to Algeria from Marseilles for years had a bomb hidden in it at this time that blew up at sea, wounding thirteen people. Officers and noncommissioned officers of the French Army, in France in official peacetime, left their barracks only armed and in groups.

The European water-skiing championship finals were held at Juan-les-Pins on the 13th.

On the 15th Jacques Soustelle, the Minister of Information in the provisional government of General de Gaulle, stopped for a traffic light in his car close to the Arc de Triomphe in Paris. Two Algerians on the sidewalk opened fire on him, one with a revolver and one with a machine gun. He managed to escape death, but three onlookers were wounded and one was killed.

On the 23rd an attempt was made to blow the top off the Eiffel Tower.

I think there may have been something atavistic about my seeking the floor of the sea at that time.

We met every morning at a restaurant; even sports were organized around food in France. Diving had become very popular; whoever was left over from the summer sooner or later turned up for it. We survivors looked, all of us, as though we were just recovering from very high fevers; beneath our tans there were new lines and circles, certain new tensions visible. We looked over-experienced, with a slightly glassy cast to our eyes, and overripe laughs. We had gone through the wringer of the Juan-les-Pins Season and now we were wiser, older; our senses had all been force-fed and now were reeling from shock, overgratification, and guilt.

One morning Mireille presented herself. "Nick. I didn't know you were a diver. I've been doing it myself off and on all summer." Her voice sounded young and wealthy. "Where have you been hiding? We looked everywhere, everywhere." And then she added, "Liliane is back."

Because she said those words to me I shall never forget Mireille. They fixed the tone of her voice, the curve of her lips, the shine of her eyes in my mind forever. I can summon her up with the greatest vividness just by recalling those words. She may be changed or dead or altered in any other way, but because it was she who happened to say "Liliane is back," she is preserved in me just as she was then.

"You look older," she went on in the same voice. "You have been enjoying yourself too much." She wagged her head slightly, teasingly. "You've been debauching, shame on you."

"You say that—"

"And I want you to meet someone. I know you will like him and he will like you. Raymond!" A dark-haired young Frenchman with a forthright expression in his eyes came up. "Nick, this is my fiancé, Raymond. Raymond, my dear friend Nick."

With all my thoughts coalescing like water changing into ice, I nevertheless had a corner of my mind still flowing enough to notice that Mireille seemed to have found someone and to be happy.

"Enchanted," I said.

"Very happy," he said.

Even the words used around her had become pretty ones.

"Much happiness," I said to them hurriedly. "Mireille, you said that Lili is back."

"Ah, you can't even wait a second for the news, can you? Well, I don't blame you and, yes, she is back. I saw her at the gala last night. She looked lov—very well." She had decided against saying "lovely," and for a good reason. Mireille had been through love and its deprivations, and all her instincts were sure on the infinitely touchy state of our feelings. If she had told me that Liliane had looked lovely when I had not been with her, I would have suffered from hearing it. It would have meant to me that I was not necessary for the realization of her beauty, and not only that but also that she had been in public radiating magnetism and I hadn't been there to fend everybody off. "*Very* well," said Mireille, as though the only interest anyone at the gala had taken in Lili had been in the state of her health.

I smiled at her, and she smiled briefly and comprehendingly back.

"Where is she staying?"

"She didn't say." Mireille was about to lapse suddenly back into the category of bitch for me when she added: "But of course I told her you were still here and I was certain you wanted to see her. She said she would be at the Victory tonight, at ten."

As I looked at Mireille wonderingly, I could feel inside myself that very slowly and deliberately and definitely the frustration that had bound me since Lili's disappearance was unraveling itself. It had been too tight for me to feel it entirely; only when I stood working myself free, talking there beside the Mediterranean lilting with morning waves, could I feel how it had been binding me.

"Nick!" Surprised and nasal, the voice of Jimmy Smoot broke in. "Are you going out today?"

"Going out!" I cried. "Out! You fool! I'm going farther out than anybody since Jacques-Yves Cousteau! Can't you see that, you clown?"

"Nick, calm down, what's the matter with you? I—"

"Never mind 'I.' *I'm* talking." Jimmy laughed nervously. "What are you doing here with those kickfins?" I went on. "Swimming home to Ardmore? What's the matter with you, Jimmy? Why are you still here? Don't you know the terrorists are after you?"

"Swimming home to Ardmore No. No, *that's* not it. Of *course* not. Oh, you're kidding. Well, stop. Be serious; this is serious, Nick. I'm filming this dive. Filming it." He flourished a case of satiny leather, unsnapped it, and drew out a motion-picture camera with many subtle and intricate adjustments. "I'm making a movie."

Slowly the convolutions of Jimmy's life began to assert their old snake-like fascination for me, and my joy was displaced for the moment by the clinical spirit of inquiry the motivations of Jimmy Smoot always brought out.

"I didn't know you had taken this up," once again losing control of the conversation to Jimmy.

"I'm learning. You learn by doing. But I always think it's easier to learn by doing if you do it with the best equipment. That's why I went to Berlin to get this camera."

"Berlin."

"Yes. I flew up."

"If you wanted a German camera you didn't have to go that far."

"I did to get *this* German camera. This isn't just any German camera. This is Kolmar's camera."

"Is that like Leica?"

He dropped his shoulders in exasperation. "Leica! Leica! Kolmar is a *photographer*, a famous German photographer. He's a Red, a Communist. Sergio put me on to him, Nick." He looked up, face puzzled, "Wasn't that awful about Sergio?"

"Terrible. Go on about the camera."

"Well. Sergio knew this famous German photographer, East German, there are two Germanies now. Kolmar is an East German. They're the Communists. I'm surprised you never heard of him. Kolmar."

"I never heard of him," I said, and then noticing the change of expression in his face I added, "but I don't know anything about photographers."

"Oh, well, people who keep up have heard of him—"

"So you bought it—"

"Black market, Nick, black market. Secretly. In *East* Berlin. In a sort of coffeehouse. It was right out of a movie. If Orson Welles had walked in I wouldn't have been surprised. It was like that, dark and full of raincoats, if you see what I mean. I never had an experience like it, never." Then he added, looking a little wistful: "I don't think I'm going to have too many more, now that Sergio's gone. I *liked* Sergio. Oh, I know, I know; you didn't think I knew but I did know. He used me. I know it, but so what. It was *exciting*, the experiences I had, the people I met—I never would have met those people, *I* never would have gone to East Berlin. Now he's gone and every day is just like every day, just like the way it was before. Dull, Nick, dull."

"He left you with this, at least, this camera. How much was it?"

He looked brightly at me, with a slight flush coming over his face. "A lot," he mumbled happily, "a lot."

He wouldn't tell me, so I was left to imagine. A thousand dollars? Two thousand dollars?

"I suppose you got the camera first, and then decided to make movies."

"What?" he said vaguely, looking toward the motor launch that would take us out to the dive.

"You got the camera and then you decided to take pictures."

"Doesn't everybody? You can't take pictures without a camera."

"I know you can't—"

"Sometimes you're awfully vague, Nick."

"I'm sorry about that."

"It's all right."

"How's Josée?"

"They're ready! We'd better get in the boat; come on, there're quite a few going and I want to be in the—what do you call the front?"

"The bow."

"I want to be in the bow so I can shoot back over the boat."

I picked up a very heavy air tank, a weight belt, literally as heavy as lead, kickfins, a face glass, and lifted them into the motor launch. Five or six others were already sitting in it.

"Salutations," said Max, a little sardonically for some reason.

"Sit next to us, Nicholas, Jimmy," said Mireille, moving closer to her fiancé. We sat down.

"How's Josée?" I said to Jimmy again.

He was sighting with his camera, and he muttered, "Just a minute. I'm preoccupied now."

Nine people got into the boat in all, and we chugged away from the wharf and out over the shining morning sea. Max was helping with the work: distributing the aqualung tanks, the belts with lead weights. He came to me. "Well, my pot, have you amused yourself since I saw you?"

"Amused myself. No, not exactly. No, not at all."

"Not still involved with that little wife of yours, are you?" He handed me the thick belt laden with many pounds of lead.

"Yes, still involved."

"You're crazy."

In spite of the strains of the summer, Max had never looked better. He had a radiant inner glow that shone through his face and body. I looked at him. "You've never been in love, have you, Max?"

He was bending over, sorting the kickfins in the bottom of the boat. Then he looked up, and his exceptional face was very close to mine. "No," he mumbled, "never."

I had been going to say, "You can't call me crazy because you don't know what you're talking about," but I held back; I had surprised the truth out of him, and I saw the confusion he lived in, so often loved, so unfeeling. He seemed like a blind man. He went on fumbling among the rubber fins at the bottom of the boat.

We arrived at the chosen spot and dropped anchor. We were about a third of a mile from shore, pointed out to sea. Cap d'Antibes was on our left, Cannes far off on the right. Behind us and between them was the bright clutter of buildings scattered over the broken hills of the French Riviera. In front was the shifting blue-green surface of the sea.

Max handed us tight-fitting rubber shirts and pants and we sprayed powder inside them so that they would slip on more easily. They were still quite hard to get into, and once in them it was very hot. I stood up. Max began to hang things on me: the weight belt, the aqualung tank. I had already put on the fins, and had my face mask in place. I put the tube from the tank into my mouth and, clumsy as an ox now, sat down slowly on the gunwale of the boat. Divers began going into the water one by one. Max glanced briefly at me, saw that I seemed to be ready, and gave me a light shove.

I put my hand up to my mask as I fell backward into the water. A cloud of bubbles rushed around my head, and the operating-room inhale-exhale of breathing under the sea began. The pressure of the water, as I began slowly pulling myself deeper, closed soundlessly in upon me, muffling my ears, pressing more and more heavily against my body from every side, and lulling my mind.

Several others had descended into the blue ahead of me; their rising bubbles hung around me like thin silver pillars. The sun spread itself mistily through this blue-and-silver world. I reached the encrusted floor and saw that a little farther on it plunged deeper, and the silver columns I was following, broken occasionally by whirling silver discs of air careening toward the surface, led down into this canyon. I pulled myself downward. The side of the canyon was rich with clusters of undersea life, sprigs of coral, red starfish here and there like Christmas bows, miniature caves and grottoes and promontories, reds and blues and greens and purples, dabs of pure colors everywhere; and as I went deeper, always more pressure closing in on me, increasing a slowly gathering woolliness in my mind, a quiet secret uncoiling, as though my mind, too, was hanging untouched by anything in a bright suspending void.

I reached the bottom of the cliff, and just below where I hung in the water two others were grouped like minnows in a puddle, busily moving forward into and backward out of a little cave. Someone else came scudding across the sea floor toward them, raising a little marine dust, and followed by a group of inquisitive fish. Now there were four of us, and four thin scintillating columns of bubbles rose from the tops of our heads up through the blue sun-shot water.

I recognized the others—Max, Mireille, and her fiancé. I was surprised to find her at this depth, dimly surprised, because here all emotions were dim ones. She hadn't seemed to me the type to do risky things. But then the depths of the sea were like the profundities of love: they revealed another person altogether, a wordless instinctual inner self who might resemble the speaking everyday person no more than a porpoise resembled a manta ray.

The four of us, encased in black rubber, hung and squirmed at the bottom of the Mediterranean, feeling close to each other because we had done this together, feeling isolated because we couldn't speak or even see each other very clearly, couldn't communicate in any way except with a few primitive gestures, like the earliest, crudest beings. It was just like love.

Liliane slowly floated toward me out of the gloom of a steep narrow canyon. "Hello," I said, hollowly, somehow, to her; "Hello," she said in an echoing voice in reply. "You've come back," I said slowly, my words reverberating from the cliffs around us; "Yes, I've come back," she answered, as she drifted closer. She was not wearing a rubber suit, and her skin had the whiteness of ivory; her black hair streamed back from her face. She was not wearing a mask either, or a tank; she was just gliding there, free. "Will you stay now?" I asked her, and she drifted a little closer so that I could see the shifting, misty lights in her eyes, and she said, "I don't know." I reached out to touch her, saying at the same time, "What do I have to do to make you stay?" A slight current carried her away from my grasp, and she said in her echoing voice, "I don't know," the current carrying her a little farther, "I don't know." She began to drift back into the dark canyon, and I thought, She is leaving me again.

I must follow her, I said slowly to myself. This time I must keep right beside her. How is it that she swims so fast? Already she is just a small white reflection at the end of that canyon, moving farther away from me. I must—

I lurched sideways. Someone was tugging my arm. Let me alone, I tried to say (but the only person I could speak to was Liliane); go away. This other person kept pulling me, and we began to rise. As we slowly came up along the encrusted face of the cliff, the water lightened from a purplish blue to a bright blue, and I saw that the person who held my arm so insistently was Mireille. I looked up and saw the two squirming shapes of the other divers far above in the vaults of the sea, and far above them was a remote bright canopy, the surface.

I'm going back, I thought regretfully. It's a long, a very long way.

And Liliane? Well, Liliane must have her own tunnel, which begins in the earth deep beneath Cap d'Antibes and leads out into the floor of the sea, and now she has drifted back into her tunnel. I should have gone with her, and saved myself this long, long climb. But I never go with her, I recalled; she always goes her own route like that; she has special ways and routes for appearing and disappearing. I couldn't breathe very well; it was so hard, took so much effort to breathe. And the surface was still remote and vague above us. It was certainly hard to get any air; it certainly was hard. Dimly a solution occurred somewhere in my mind: air, air. There was more air somewhere; let's see, where was it? In the tank, where the other was. Then why am I not getting it? Because it was separate in the tank, it was a reserve. Then the lever that released the reserve occurred to me, and with my free hand I reached around and pulled it. New air rushed through the tube into my mouth. I gulped it, filled myself with it, and my brain slowly began to clear: it too had been very deeply submerged, and now a few shafts of light broke through into it and I began to see what had happened.

When we reached the surface next to the boat, in the warm, used, superficial water of the surface, Mireille took out her mouthpiece and said, "You were very peculiar down there. What were you trying to get hold of?"

"Nothing," I said, "nothing."

"You had a touch of the rapture of the deep, no?"

"The rapture," I said, "yes."

We climbed clumsily up the ladder into the boat, were relieved of our tanks of air and fins, and I slowly and with great effort peeled off the black rubber suit. Once out of it I sat down in the bow, and stared. Mireille handed me some chocolate as an energy restorer; I needed it. I had very little energy left; I had lost it, left it on the floor of the sea. It was still there, in ransom to the mermaid, the water nymph; rather to a hallucination from a temporary oversupply of nitrogen in my brain and spine. I might have known that that's where Liliane had been hiding. I should have looked there before.

"You were very strange," Mireille said, shaking her clammy locks, stripped once again to her bikini. "Very odd. How do you feel now?"

"I'm all right."

"Let me sit with you a moment, until you're sure."

"Your fiancé is a good diver."

"Do you like him?"

"Yes."

"Yes," she said in a tone reflecting long thoughts behind it, nodding. "Yes, he's very nice. Do you know who he is?"

"He's—you said his name was Roger?"

"Raymond. But do you know who he is? You remember the boy from Paris I told you about, I threw him out of my apartment?" She looked at me closely, twinklingly. "Jewish?"

"Is this—"

"Same boy." She shrugged happily. "I can't help it; he overpowered me." Mireille turned to face me. "You were right, I am Jewish. You see—he came back to my apartment the day I suppose after you and I went to the night club—he just barged in and demanded, 'What's the matter with you, anyway?' He just stood there, like God, hands on his hips, and said, 'What's the matter with you, anyway?' And I sat blinking and beginning to shake, feeling in danger as though I were going to fall into a void, and finally I said, 'What do you mean?' and my voice squeaked at the end and I saw that something terrible was about to happen. 'You didn't get mad the other night because I was *Jewish*, did you?' he said, demanded as a matter of fact, frowning at me with those eyes. It was the way he said it—Jewish—as though he were saying Swiss or Catholic or anything else; the word began to change in my mind while I was standing there staring and shaking. And I—well, I *accepted* it; I didn't just accept it; I liked it, I *loved* it, if you want to know the real truth, and all because he said the word, he said it, about himself, and in that tone, that way. Well," and she sighed and handed me another piece of chocolate.

Jimmy came up. "I got you as you surfaced," he said to me.

"How did I look?"

"Swell. You never looked better."

"I've got to give Raymond some of this chocolate," Mireille said, and moved toward the other end of the boat.

"Yes, you never looked better. I hope it came out. I hope they all came out because I'm leaving, at last, leaving. Tomorrow, I think. That Eiffel Tower business was too much, the end. I *like* to go to the top of the Eiffel Tower. I might have been up there!"

"They found the bomb before it went off."

"That's not very comforting. I'm getting out of here just as soon as they can get me on a plane. Not a boat. They bombed one of the boats!"

"I know. What about Josée?"

"Finished, if you want to know, all through. It wasn't real *real* love. Not quite real. She was partially interested in me for my passport. How do you like that! It's true. Partially interested in me for my passport. I just got thoroughly disillusioned; I started to *see through* her one day, the day that gas place in Nice blew up. I'd been begging her for weeks to get her papers, and then that place blew up and I bawled her out for being so slow, and she said—do you know what she said, Nick?"

He would not have told me until I answered, so I said, "No, what did she say?"

"She said, 'That's why I'm marrying you, so a man will help with things like this in my life.' How do you like that!"

"How did she say this? She doesn't speak English."

"She does now," he said vaguely; "she took lessons this summer, four hours a day. She could speak English."

"Where is she now?"

"I don't know, Nick, I've got something to tell you. It's so sordid. I'm blushing just to think. It's so sordid. Who else speaks English in this boat?"

"Just Mireille. She can't hear."

"This aunt of Josée's came to see her here, to be with her, supposedly, to chaperon her, to protect her. Very respectable and all that, and they took me in. I supported that aunt here for weeks. Do *you* know what she really came here for? Brace yourself. She wanted an a-bor-tion. An abortion! What kind of people are they? *She wanted an abortion!* Josée's a nurse. Did I tell you that?"

"No."

"Josée's a nurse, and this aunt thought Josée knew some doctor who would do it for her. Can you imagine! An abortionist in Ardmore!"

"*Josée* wasn't giving the abortion, or getting it either, for that matter. How did you find out about this?"

"She told me." He was looking into his camera.

"That was very honest."

"Nick, I was past all that. I *saw through* her even more. I moved right away, to a little place in Cagnes; she'll never find me there. I wouldn't've come here today, to tell the truth, but I've got to do this movie. I've got to have some of it done, anyway, before I go home. I've been in Europe for about a year. I call it my Career Year. I like that, don't you? Career Year."

"Career Year."

"And so I had to have one, you know, a career, by the time I go home. That was the way we agreed, my father and me. Time is getting pretty short, and since I already had this camera, it was obvious. Take pictures."

"How are they coming out so far?"

"Not very good yet, Nick. Mostly glares and shadows so far, and a lot of film doesn't seem to have anything on it. This camera's so good, I don't think I'm exactly up to it yet. But I've got to have something to show my father, got to." He worked over it, frowning: "Go over to the other side of the boat, will you? Here, take this mask. Sit over there and start adjusting the strap or something. Let's see, let's see," as he bent over the camera, "six point four . . . three hundredth . . . if only it wasn't in *German . . . Xenoplan!* What in the world can that be! . . . Oh, fooey. Smile, Nick, here goes, smile!"

162

IIIIIIIIIIIIIIIIIII

That evening crept over Juan-les-Pins more deliberately and more subtly than any other. I watched it from my window, studied the sky as it meditatively deepened its blueness and the sea of pines as it slowly settled from late-afternoon waving into the attentive immobility of nightfall. Cap d'Antibes, which had during the day something of a night club's facelessness, acquired as evening deepened a night club's gathering festiveness, a twinkle here and a sparkle there, lively lights in clusters and in winking isolation, a sense of movement and of people dressing up and of music stirring. I had left the radio on, unheard; it slowly wove itself into what I was watching. A liquid-voice lady in Paris talked calmly about something for a while, and then a wistful accordion played songs about the sea, and the river Seine and so on, the peculiar French songs, the one about the lover who is not an angel and the one about the crook who shouldn't go out tonight. The music wove itself into the evening, and I heard without listening and watched without seeing as the decisive night of my life closed slowly around me.

Of course she would come. If she said that she would come, then she would come.

Why did I want her to come?

I sat with my hands folded in my lap and looked down at them. I wanted her because she was all I had. I had come here to get away from her, to find a bigger and finer and more beautiful love, and I had not found it. I was left once again with Liliane, and Liliane's love was smaller than what I dreamed of.

But I was left with hers. My hands tightened with a minute convulsion: I was inevitably left with her love, because her love was all I was capable of. I wasn't capable of anything better. Nowhere would love be more findable than here, you would think, and yet I had not found it.

The love you get can only be as big as you are. And I was only as big as Liliane's intense but unstable, unfaithful love for me. That was all I was up to. The most that can be hoped for from love is that it will stretch you; everybody gets the love he deserves.

I sat without moving in the chair. I stopped thinking then by a furious command of the will. The evening was no longer watched; I looked at it. The heard music I listened to. I waited without moving for ten o'clock.

At nine forty-five I got up from the chair. I happened to have on some brown pants and a white sports shirt and the espadrilles. I didn't change, didn't dress for an evening out at Juan-les-Pins, didn't brush my hair, didn't prepare, didn't think. I went.

I got to the Victory, and sat down at a table on the terrace. Sergio's father, a worn old man, sat down with me. He started to talk immediately about Sergio. He was still in shock from having been robbed and deserted by his son, and he assumed that everyone in the world was thinking and talking of nothing else but that. I had completely forgotten about it, and now I heard him talking as if from a distance. "He worked hard, my son. Hard. From six in the morning to ten, eleven, twelve at night! Seven days a week. From May to October. He did that for eight years now. And you know what happened? It was too much for him. All that work, and that" —his vague eyes then surprisingly flashed with venom—"rotten fiancée of his, that rotten convent girl! Worthless, worthless. Had to have money, had to have her own house! Her own house! What young people have their own house here! I ask you! None! It was too much for my boy, too much, too much. That work. That fiancée. And you, you too, for example." He looked speculatively at me, a certain twinkling speculation in his eyes, as though he were my admirer or murderer. "You rich strangers who come here with your cars to amuse yourselves for a season. You are too much for the youth here. You turn their heads. They want a car, they want a different girl every night, they want twenty sweaters. All right. Then you know what happens? They get to know one of you, two of you, five of you, and they find out you're all gangsters. They find out you made your money some evil way, some evil way. It doesn't look so hopeless to them then. They begin to understand. So *that's* how it's done, they think. You're all gangsters. Go on, admit it," he was smiling disturbingly at me, "admit it. I don't care. Admit it."

"I'm very sorry about Sergio; I think his nerves got the better of him."

"Yes, yes, his nerves, his nerves," and he sighed a long shaking sigh as he lifted himself out of the chair; then he stopped and looked down on me with that light in his eye and that pitying smile, shaking his head, "Gangsters, smart young gangsters . . ." and he went off toward the kitchen.

After a while Liliane came down the street toward me. She was wearing a pink dress and wore a thin, shiny and light-colored coat over it. She looked solitary, energetic, slim, tanned, moist, nervous, willful, calculating, courageous, idealistic, vulnerable, explosive, and she also looked one other thing: she looked like a possession of mine. I saw her very clearly and completely. Neither love nor hate is blind; they're the most clear-sighted states in the world. Your lover and your worst enemy often see your deepest qualities, your hidden seam of value, your speck of divinity. No one else has the urgent emotions necessary to do this.

I got up and came forward, and we met under the little wooden arch at the entrance of the Victory. It was not unlike my vision at the bottom of the Mediterranean, my rapture, my rapture of the deep. I said "Hello" and so did she, and I said something about her having been away, and she said something about it. We began to walk along the promenade by the sea, away from the center of Juan-les-Pins.

To say to her, as we moved hesitatingly along the dark promenade, rather empty now too toward the end of September, that I loved and wanted her in spite of the fact that she was not worthy of me, and because of the fact that I was not worthy of what I conceived myself potentially to be either, to say that wasn't possible; it was equally impossible to say the reverse, which was true: that I was not worthy of what she herself might be or might have been. I lacked the emotional courage and she lacked the fidelity to be what we might have been, and so we could do no better than each other; but to say that was impossible too. It was possible to say how much I loved and needed her but I—lacked the courage. Hate is not the opposite of love; in fact, they closely resemble each other in many ways. The opposite of love is fear, love's opposite and greatest enemy.

"How was your trip?"

"Lovely. At least at first it was. Then it got—" She lost interest in telling me whatever it was that it then got. "I don't suppose you missed me at all?"

"Of course I missed you. That's all I did while you were away— I—"

"No, it's all right, never mind. We're past politeness."

"Who's being polite! What do you suppose I felt when you disappeared like that? My wife suddenly disappearing."

"Relief. I'm sure that's what you felt, and you were right. You came here to get away from me."

"Well, I didn't get away from you. I couldn't. I can't."

"I know it's necessary for you to, because I'm not worthy of y—"

"What!"

"I'm not. I know that. I know . . . what I am, now," she said very quietly.

"You know what you—!"

"I know. I'm hopeless for you. You can't have a wife like me. I know that. And I cannot seem to change. I can't." She stopped and turned. There was a little illumination here; I saw her face. "I'm going to marry Marc because he is older, much older than you are, and he's unbelievably cynical about anything good—it's all because of the Occupation and people he was responsible for having killed —you needn't hear the whole ghastly story. I heard it quite a few times during our trip. The important thing is that an unfaithful wife," there was just a lightning interruption in the beat of the sentence as she said the word, "will remind him every day how worthless all the rest of the human race is, and that will make him feel better about himself." She looked almost brightly at me, in the eyes for the first time. "So I suit him," she touched my face, "I don't suit you. I'm so sorry." She was crying, and I stared transfixed at her, "Goodbye!" She ran awkwardly back toward the remaining late-September lights and rhythm of Juan-les-Pins.

I started after her, but then my thinking began to cave in again, the way it had done in Paris. I began to think that I was still two hundred feet down in the Mediterranean and that I could only move slowly, slowly, with all those tons of water surrounding me and pressing down on me. I began to run after her, but everything in my head had become slow, so numbed by this burdensome pressure, this irresistible weight pressing from all sides that I was not making much headway. I fought my way forward, but slowly, slowly.

I eventually found myself in my apartment, and got into bed. I can't keep thinking this way, I thought. I'm falling apart again. How many kings of France can I name? Napoleon Third, Louis-Phillippe, Charles the Tenth, Louis Eighteenth—I think I've missed somebody—Louis Sixteenth, Fifteenth, Fourteenth—now it's just Louises all the way to—to Henry the Fourth? François the Second? I forgot Napoleon the Great. Not a king but an emperor, but I'll count him anyway. He comes of course between Louis the Sixteenth and Louis the Eighteenth. This isn't working.

I'll write a poem, in my head. About the circus, for instance. The jugglers, or the tightrope walkers. Yes.

The tightrope walker

Yes, what else? What's he doing?

The tightrope walker is tired
Because he

Why would he be tired? Just walking a short distance like that? Why would he be?

The tightrope walker is tired
Because he

There could only be one reason, couldn't there?

> *The tightrope walker is tired*
> *Because he must always lean forward*
> *To weave the rope.*

There. I guess it isn't a poem. Still, it makes sense.

|||||||||||||||||||||||

The next morning—I didn't notice the weather—I went ahead doing the simplest actions, making coffee, spreading marmalade on a *croissant,* despite an unbalancing lathe-like spinning inside my head. It felt as though it would continue until I came to the end of the chain of simple physical actions that I had begun. I didn't know when I would reach the end or what it was. I went ahead: out of the door, down the stairs, down the street to buy the newspaper. I sat down in a café I'd never gone to before and tried to read it, but every story, even one about a ceramic exhibition, filled me with alarm. I left the paper there and went back to the apartment.

There was a letter in the mailbox. It had come by hand.

DEAR FRIEND:

Excuse me for having left so abruptly, but perhaps you can understand my grief.

I crouched down and resting my forearms on my knees tried to read the rest:

I need one final assistance from you, who have always been kind to me. I give you a rendezvous at the Café of the Station tonight at nine o'clock. I will understand if you think it better not to come.

Best thoughts,

and the signature. Unintelligible. It was not Lili. It was Jeannot. I realized now that the letter was in his handwriting.

168

My head continued to keep me off balance by this peculiar sensation of something turning inside.

It was nine-thirty. I went out again and got into my car. The De la Croies would be up by now, and if they weren't I would get them up.

I drove very fast through Juan-les-Pins, at a speed that would have killed fifty or a hundred people a month earlier, and tore along the narrow, twisting Cap d'Antibes road, with its many blind turns. Fortunately, Alfa-Romeos are made by and for impassioned Italians.

Their driveway suddenly came up, and I careened into it, skidded across the gravel, and then, gaining headway again, shot down the drive and stopped with another skid beside the house.

Titou was on the open terrace, holding a large cup of coffee, wearing only a bikini, looking very thin and very tanned, and very amused. "Nick, what are you doing, you idiot! You're leading the Tour de France, eh? Well, you made a wrong turn, back there at the driveway. This way is the Mediterranean Sea. All right?"

I came up to him on the terrace. We shook hands and I said: "How are you? How was the trip? You look well. Where's Liliane?"

"Very funny welcome. Have some coffee. Monique!" The maid came. *Café au lait pour Monsieur. Merci.* Sit down, Nicholas Petrovich. You look strange. Russian. I begin to see that Russian part of you now. What are you trying to be, Dostoevsky? Look at yourself —well there's no mirror here, but I'm your mirror and I'm telling you that your hair is standing in all directions, you are barefoot, which is not permitted after the first of September on the Côte d'Azur, those brown pants haven't been pressed ever, that white shirt isn't, and let me see, let me see," turning me, "um, the rest is mostly your face. You might have shaved this morning, don't you think? Your eyes, though, what are they so—so—"

I jerked away from him. "Where is Liliane?"

"All right, all right. Of course. Liliane is staying on the boat, in the port of Antibes. You heard, you know about—about her plan to marry my uncle. Yes, of course. Well, my pal, my old crazy pal, listen to me, listen." He looked at me closely. "Is it all right? You'll permit me to say something, something about Liliane?" I nodded. "It's that she is, Liliane is what we in French call *hysterique*. Um. It does not mean hysterical."

I looked back at him nakedly. "I love her."

"Come, Nick," he put his arm around me, "sit here. What if we don't talk about love this morning? It's like, you understand, cancer as a topic for me. It's important, yes, but I can do nothing about it. It's better for you to put your mind off it for a little while. Here's your coffee." And then he went off into a swift dialogue with the maid over what kind of bread there was, what size, hot or cold, what sort of jam she had to go with it—one of the Penelope's-knitting conversations about the details of details that only the most intelligent French can sustain.

When every last decision had finally been reached, she left. Titou instantly returned with equal intensity to the discussion of love and cancer. "But I tell you," he continued, "you really want her."

"I do, yes."

"My uncle leads a rather dangerous life." He stirred his coffee noisily. "Rather dangerous. You don't know. By the time Liliane is free to marry him, you don't know."

"What are you trying to say? I've got to find Lili. I'm going to that boat. What's the name of it?"

"The *Fidèle*," he said instantly. "The *Fidèle Trois*, three."

"The *Fidèle*," I repeated savagely to myself.

"It or she or him or whatever you say in English is long and white and a sailing yacht. Stylish, expensive, we rented him in Cannes. It's not going to sail away this morning. It's not, and so you have some minutes to hear about my uncle. It is important."

"Go ahead."

Right away I wished I hadn't said that. Titou did not "go ahead" in conversation. He thought it crude and un-French to do so. And so he took a while explaining to me how blunt and American I'd become, and in the end I had to more or less apologize to him for having said "Go ahead" before he would.

"Well, then," he went on, "my uncle really would prefer to die some of these days. I think so. He would prefer if his life ended because it would," he searched for the thought and the word, "make him feel better. It's true! He's ruined since the wartime affair, certainly since the end of the Occupation. He's better dead, so he thinks. Well, but one can't put oneself to death—my uncle can't, at least. He's too proud; it would be confessing everything, admitting to the world that the world was right about him, that he *agreed* with them about himself." He leaned forward, his busy face concentrating on me. "He will never do it. But! Somebody else might, some of these days."

"If somebody had been going to kill him for the things that happened in the war, they would have done it years ago."

"That is true, but now we are once again in France at a 1940, a—that wonderful phrase you have in America, a fork in the road. I thought that was the most curious expression I heard in America. When two roads go apart it doesn't look anything like a *fork*. Still, there you are! And we are there in France, at the fork. Will we go to the Right with the parachutists, or to the Left with democracy? You know which way my uncle wants to go. And with my uncle, he doesn't merely sit and *want* in these times. He acts. He of course loathes De Gaulle and wishes for the defeat of the new Constitution that we are going to vote about. There are very few like my uncle, if you ask me! He thinks the Bourbons were a bit too liberal. He has his friends all the same, and he had his meetings on this cruise; we went to North Africa, did you know that? Yes, and in fact the real purpose of the trip, I gradually found out, was so that my uncle could mix himself with everything that was going on there, see if there were many leftover Fascists like himself knocking around the streets of Algiers, and in general stir things up! Yes, whole blocs of new enemies were made! By the handfuls! My uncle's program is to drop parachutists on Paris, shoot most of the politicians, send General de Gaulle to Martinique to do his memoirs again, send all of the Army to Algeria and wipe out the rebellion with Nazi tactics —you understand, obliterate an entire village if one rebel soldier is

171

recruited from it, shoot a hundred civilians for every French soldier killed. Like that. That is my uncle's program, in its broad aspect. He explained it to lots of people in Algeria. Anybody can become a leader of those desperate *colons* there, even somebody like my uncle. Who can tell? And so he would be important again, important enough to be either revenged or killed, and I think that he wants only one or the other."

Titou's droll French eyes then turned more thoughtful. "You tant enough to be either revenged or killed, and I think that he *is*. But he wasn't always. He was once an idealist."

I gave a kind of wild laugh.

"No, he was. He still is. It's true, Nicholas Petrovich. He worships excellence, and that's his ideal. Look at him himself. He's fifty years of age, and he looks thirty-eight? Thirty-six? Because he has always done everything right for his body. He couldn't endure to get less than the best out of it. He is brilliant, he understands *nuclear physics*. He studied it in jail as soon as he heard about the atomic bomb. He studied *space*. Space. There is where the future is going, and my uncle wanted to understand that. It's a curve always expanding in essence, or something like that, he told me. He knows more about Russia and Communism than you, Nicholas Petrovich, even *suspect*. Do you know who assassinated Czar Alexander the Second and how old he was and what the girl was like who gave the assassin the signal to throw the bomb when the Czar got out of his carriage to investigate the *first* bomb next to the something canal in St. Petersburg in 1882 I think it was and why they did it? No. Uncle knows. Do you know about Axelrod? Of course not. Uncle knows. He had to have an excellent mind, that's all. Excellence is the only thing in the universe he admires. He's terribly antireligious because he can't understand God creating so many inferior, un-excellent people. We don't get along too well, my uncle and I, in case you failed to notice, and that is because I do not happen to be excellent. He has contempt for me, affectionate contempt. I know it. He can't help it.

"*He* thinks France is the most excellent thing in the history of the world. He thinks France is the most *brilliant,* the most cultivated, gifted, *sweet,* elegant, splendid country that ever was. Um-hum. So. And now there is—was the Fourth Republic giving away our glorious Empire and our glorious leadership of Europe and our glorious mission to teach everybody else how to civilize themselves. He hated it. He hated the Third Republic too. He *loved* Pétain. Excellence, the old virtues, traditional military honor, all that. Democracy is all mediocrity to my uncle. All those politicians in Paris *toying* with France. It drove him crazy.

"He isn't in favor of De Gaulle because he thinks that De Gaulle is too realistic. I said before, Uncle is a pure idealist.

"People do what they *want* in a democracy. Nobody forces them to be excellent. Uncle is against democracy, and that is why. People must be forced to excel, he thinks. Forced all the time. Only the ones who become really excellent ought to be allowed to have any power.

"And then, when he betrayed those people during the Occupation he suddenly began to suspect that he wasn't excellent either, not really, not at the deepest core, and I don't think he could ever forgive himself for that. He eats himself up because of that. So he just sprays out poison into the atmosphere all the time, and he hunts around for death." Shaking his head a little regretfully and rapidly stirring his coffee, Titou added, "That's the way he is."

"This doesn't have anything to do with me and Liliane."

"It has everything to do with Liliane. I am talking about her future husband."

"No, you're not." I stood up and walked toward the house. "Where is he? I'm going to tell him that."

"Oh, he's not here," said Titou automatically. "He's on the boat."

||||||||||||||||||

In the car I couldn't control my foot, and I rocketed across Cap d'Antibes like a torpedo aimed for the hull of the *Fidèle,* tearing along the top of the old wall, skidding into a steep little street, through an archway and into the port. There was only one yacht; it was a sailing yacht, it was white. I stopped the car beside it. Across the stern was written, not *Fidèle*—that must have been Titou's idea of an amusing substitution—but *Flèche de Corse*.

I sprang up the little gangplank and onto the deck. Lili came up from below, wearing white trousers and a bright blouse. She also had on plain gold earrings that somehow in themselves stunned me by the change they made in her, revealing another way of life, another culture she had abruptly lent herself to, another Liliane.

"Nick," she began with a sad frown, "why are you bursting in here? What—"

"Get off this boat. Off. Where's Marc?"

"He's not here," she said with an incredulous look.

I went down the ladder and ran into Marc just stepping into the passage. He looked very surprised to see me. He was tanned and wearing white. He did not know quite what to make of me.

"You're holding my wife here by force," I said a little crazily.

"Liliane is and always will be as free as one of these gulls in the port," he replied quietly, "as you know."

"You're forcing her to stay here—"

"Are you sick? What's the matter with you?"

"—and I'm taking her away. You've been holding—"

Liliane seized one of my arms. "Nick! Nicholas!"

Without shaking myself free I looked across at Marc and I said, "I'm going to kill you."

Even then I did not mean what I said. It was pure instinctive cruelty, an inspiration created by hate. If he longed for death I would tantalize him with it. "You're going to leave here!" I said to Liliane. The three of us were practically on top of each other in the cramped passage.

"Nick, please, please!" Lili cried, clinging to my arm.

"Leave here, leave now!"

"Come up to the deck, I can't stand . . ."

"How could you ever breathe the air here—"

"You have just made a threat against my life, as I will remind you. That is a criminal offense specifically able to be punished by the law. Now you are childishly falling down to petty insults, which does not surprise me. You are childish, I find," he said with concentration, "aren't you?"

"Marc," she said, "I beg you."

"Of course your marriage is over, finished! She prefers marriage to me. However much she must amuse herself elsewhere."

I saw her eyes flash at him then with a look of blind hopeless confusion in them, and then she turned away. The two of us who claimed to love her at last noticed her. I went after her up to the deck. "Go away," she said wearily, "I beg you. Please."

"Lili," I said rapidly, "I won't go, I'm sorry that I—"

"You've done nothing. It was me, my fault always. Didn't I tell you? I only suit *him.*" She looked at Marc with a cold blank comprehending stare. He gazed opaquely back at her. "Don't you see it now?" she said.

"Lili!"

"You would always be crying if I were there, always. Go away, darling, I'm just an invalid; think of me that way. I only suit *him;* can't you see it now? Can't you?"

Somehow I found myself off the *Flèche de Corse* later on, driving into the mountains.

IIIIIIIIIIIIIIIIII

I drove all day. The car under those hours of combustion in that unwavering sunlight slowly became a caldron as I roared up some steep curving road into the Maritime Alps. At one point I noticed that the rubber holding the windshield in place was beginning to melt. Waves of heat poured up through the floor and down over the windshield. My sun-conditioned face was burned again; the seat was hot enough to singe. On and up I roared, the car seeming to get stronger from all I demanded of it, to "break in" all over again to full utility; full-throated and searing, it shot ahead toward the peaks. Holding the wheel I possessed the special control of such cars; I was not driving it, I was a part of it; it did not respond to me, we acted together.

When now and then my eyes flickered away for a second from the road wriggling snake-like beneath us, I received an impression of groves of little trees, blue-barked trees they were, with pink blossoms: not an illusion. Hanging in a crevice of some mountain many miles off there would be a small pile of orange cubes, village roofs, tucked away. Then the vegetation changed: groves of olives like blue-gray clouds hovered on the mountainsides. There was a terrible stillness; an old crumbling castle across a steep ravine focused the surrounding silence. Occasionally I burst into a village and wrenched with the car around the church while everyone stopped to stare at this event. I tore on into the highlands, moist green meadows swung among the mountain shoulders, with fresh water in deep troughs hurrying through them, and a tilting instability everywhere.

I couldn't stop anywhere, because then all the hate I felt would catch up to me; as long as I was so fused with the car, taken up with fighting to survive in the car, then I was away from it.

The land abruptly changed again; slabs of gray rock reared monumentally up, and I went twisting through rocky funnels upward; beside me a smoky blue stream hurtled down toward the sea. Then all that was left behind, just as the meadows, villages, olives, and blue trees and everything else had been.

Open meadows again, the final peaks, rounded. I was on a gravel road; there was little except the intense blue Mediterranean sky above me; water rippled nearby here and there. The road ended; I stopped. In front of me was a final frail tongue of snow, the survivor of everything the heat of summer could inflict. It was a very pathetic patch of snow, looking as though it had been through a long illness or else perhaps as though it had been through a summer at Juan-les-Pins. I feel like that snow looks, I thought. That's what love can do to you.

Sitting in the cooling car, marooned, as the sun went behind the mountain apex in front of me, shooting splendor around the peak for a little while and immediately throwing shadows over the highest fields, I felt the wind lifting. It twirled through the car and moved something scratchily on the floor. It was a piece of paper, the letter I'd got this morning. Jeannot. Nine o'clock tonight. *You who have always been kind to me . . . I will understand if you think it better not to come.*

I started the motor, which was like a detonation in this huge empty mountain field, turned around, and began to descend.

Darkness was closing rapidly over Nice as I approached it along a straight highway where car after car sped past in the other direction: "*Going* somewhere," I heard from each one as it went by, "*Going* somewhere." Nice was busy and crowded at the evening rush hour, half lighted, police controlled. A convoy of soldiers rolled through the busiest section at the busiest moment, a dun-colored heavy procession in this gaudy city where parades usually consisted of people throwing flowers at each other.

I drove on along the sea with many other cars and scooters and motorcycles and trucks and bicycles. At the intersection of two highways a policeman standing in a white shaft of spotlight elegantly directed traffic with white gloves and a white stick. Other police with flashlights gestured nervously from the sidelines. Everyone was hurrying; it was just a normal Nice nightfall, but there was an urgency, as in an evacuation, about the way these city workers hurried through the closing-in darkness to get home.

At Juan-les-Pins it was completely dark. The Café of the Station, the blank one next to the railroad station, was dim and empty. I stood at the bar and ordered coffee. Across the street the loud, open café was tuning up. Nothing happened. Twenty minutes later I glimpsed Jeannot outside. He gestured, and I paid and went out. By now he was halfway down the street. At the corner he turned right. I at last caught up with him at the National Highway.

"Hey, wait!" I said, grabbing him by the shoulders. "What is all this?"

He turned—we were under the highway streetlight—and despite the new, distant look of his face he smiled and said, "It's like that when you're behind the enemy's lines."

"Now that you've led me to the busiest highway in the South of France under the streetlight, are you satisfied?"

"Ah!" a mock contemptuous Mediterranean gesture of the hand and head, "always a talker, you were. You're going to go on talking when I'm gone?"

"Gone? I don't know."

"Ah, you."

"I didn't know you were going anywhere. Where are you going?"

He nodded several times, as though to himself. "I'm going, yes, I'm going."

We started walking up the National Route, plunging quickly into the blackness beneath the old trees. "Home?"

He took a long, tremulous breath. "Home."

"Are you going to get into trouble there, is that what you're going to do?"

"One will see."

"But I won't see! How will I ever see? You're going and then that's it, goodbye. I'll never see."

"Wasn't it funny, the day I found you washing the car? That was droll! How long ago was that?"

"About two months ago."

"No! It's not possible! Only two?"

"I thought you wanted to steal the car."

"What! You thought that? Ah, that now, that's not nice, not at all nice. I excuse myself, eh, but there you wrong me. Steal your car! What do y—"

"Jeannot, Jeannot, I didn't *know* you at all."

"All the same, it's not nice, not at all."

"I thought—I thought you were a Spaniard, remember? You told me you were a Spaniard then."

"Yes, that's true. Filthy race, the Spaniards."

"Listen . . ."

"Yes?"

"Listen. Stop a minute. Don't go to Algeria. You understand? Don't go. I'll sponsor you, or whatever it is, in America. Don't. That war there, tortures, the way they kill, the interrogations. Don't. I'll arrange something so you can come to America. Okay? Come on, you can say that. Like an American. Try. Okay?"

He was smiling distantly; his eyes glittered briefly at me. "Now that," he said softly, "that's very good. You are a fine guy. I embrace you for that." He kissed me methodically on both cheeks. "I cannot go to America," he added quietly.

After a silence I said, "When will you leave?"

"Tomorrow."

"Tomorrow."

"I am sorry to leave. I admit it. I tell you something. I loved France. Yes. They were nice to me here, many people were, nice. And it's a wonderful country, I admit it. They are very advanced, very advanced. I was happy here, I was *learning*, and seeing things I had never seen before; I was learning, and some people were very nice to me. I felt, to tell the truth, as though when I was over there in Algeria I was sitting on a big hill and far away there was a train going by, and I was sitting still on top of that hill. But here in France I was *on* the train, yes, I was moving, I was seeing, I was going ahead. And then, ah"—a deep, guttural stomach-groan—"what do you want, this war, the parachutists, my—my—" He stopped himself forcibly.

"What—What was it you said we had to see each other about? You said in your note—"

"Yes, of course, it was, let's see, it was . . . Just a moment." He was silent for a little. "It was money, yes."

"I owe you some money, when you went away like that—"

"You'll forgive me?"

"I forgive you."

We figured out what money I owed him, and I gave him some more.

"But in any case," he said sternly, "you didn't think I would have left without bidding you goodbye."

"No, I didn't think that."

"No." A silence. "And you, what will you do now?"

"I'll have to go back to work soon, and earn some money."

"What is your work, by the way?"

Typical of Juan-les-Pins that I had never had occasion to mention anything as neutral as work all summer. "I import products of France into America."

"*Very* good."

"Sometimes."

"I will go with you to America some time when you go! I want to see New York and the Far West! Sure, I—"

"You . . . ?"

He was silent.

"Jeannot, don't go to Algeria! I beg you. There's nothing to be done. Your father is *dead!*" His breath hissed sharply as though from the jab of a needle. "Yes, yes, he is dead! He will *not* come back! He does not want you to die, don't you see? No! You are supposed to live! You can't bring him back! The tortures there, please, you're crazy. 'Vengeance is mine, says the Lord'—"

"I never heard that said."

"It's not Moslem," I said hurriedly, "but it's true, true!"

"That would astonish me."

"Don't go! It would be the end of you!"

He nodded slowly to himself.

"Well then, well then," I said a little disconnectedly, "this is quite a day in my life. I've got nobody, nobody at all; well, then, this is it; nobody at all, nobody at all, nobody."

He patted me slowly on the back, but he didn't say anything. "I have to go," he said finally in a low, almost apologetic voice.

I stood in front of him, looking carefully into his eyes. "You are courageous, aren't you? That's what you are, isn't it? Courageous."

"Not courageous. No. I am not. I feel deeply in my heart,

though, deeply. I have to do what I feel there. Everybody does, it's natural. Everybody does."

Then, quietly, he left me, walking with that slight lilt away into the black night, turning just before the lamplight abandoned him and with his raised hand giving me a short, a somehow cheerful, a quick and buoyant salute.

"Wait a minute, Jeannot! Wait a minute!"

"Yes," he called out of the darkness, "What?"

"I wanted to tell you . . . you are . . . well loved here. Did you know that?"

"Happy," he called in a voice he kept control of, "I am happy for that. Happy."

A truck came by, and when its roar had faded he could not be heard any more. I turned and walked alone back down the National Route. Occasionally a huge truck or a tiny car went by. But Juan-les-Pins, the beach branch of the town of Antibes, was as dead as a flower at the end of its season. I was by myself. I turned off the highway and started down a black street under the trees toward the beach.

The lamps along the beach promenade were illuminated, which made it all more abandoned-looking. I walked past the flower beds, the palm trees, the statue, past a sunken, gloomy courtyard—Liliane and I had danced there when it was all cha-cha-cha and bamboo—past the ghost hotels and soaped-over restaurants, on down the windy promenade to the place where I had parked my car, got in, and without a backward glance or thought drove like a fugitive from justice to the De la Croies.

They were at dinner. The dining room was a medium-sized, gracefully oval, lightly orangish, as though it had been carved inside a peach. A few wall lights scattered a mutely festive glow over the optimistically yellow tablecloth, the red and green flowers, and the four tanned people, brightly dressed, seated around the table.

They had reached the cheese and coffee. Titou had been talking loudly, and was leaning over to squeeze Liliane's arm. Opposite him Constance was looking with serene, humorous interest at Marc, who was saying something critical and amusing about whatever Titou had been saying. I had heard Titou's words during the several seconds it took to cross from the front door to the dining room, but since I knew they could not concern me and would no longer concern them as soon as I appeared, I didn't listen.

When I entered, still in the brown pants and white shirt, still barefoot and uncombed and unshaved, silence fell over the table with concert precision. They all gazed up with fluctuating expressions at me, and then Marc said, in a rich, entertained voice reinforced by the silence it entered, "He's come to kill me, what do you think of that?" The others started swiftly to have their second reaction, but Marc cut in: "Yes, yes, he's come to kill me. But you're late, my dear man, late. We've reached the *cheese*. Twenty minutes earlier and you would have found the carving knife just here, on the table, very conveniently at hand, very conveniently. But now, this?" With a puckered smile he held up a frail little cheese carver. "For me? I am sorry, but no, no. It will require more than that, far more."

"What on earth—" Constance stared at him, clutching the edge of the table.

"Threatened my life, yes, he did, this morning, on the yacht. Isn't that so, Lili?"

Lili sat very still in her chair, looking smaller than she was.

"You threatened him?" said Constance on a rising note to me.

I had forgotten that I had—who cared about *him?*—but remembering, I said, "Yes. I threatened him."

"And how dare you, *you*, how do you dare to threaten my brother, will you please tell me?"

"Your brother isn't worth—"

"How have you, who aren't even—even anything, not French, not Russian, not American, some little businessman, some refugee, how have you the presumption to do this in our country? Answer me, please!"

I gazed abstractly at her, shaking my head negatively.

"Answer me, please, and then get out of this house. Titou—"

"Mother, please, Mother, Nick—"

"Liliane," I said gently, touching her throat, "are you ready?" She did not stir.

"What else can he do, poor refugee, but threaten? What else? It isn't as though he had any importance in any field, not as though he were someone of some standing, even financial, even political, even social, anything. Just a wanderer, after all, so what can one expect of him? Look," he then said in a new tone, "you, get out."

I then realized that if Liliane did not soon act, I might do what he was goading me to do; I was only human, and not only that, I was a Russian human.

"Liliane?" I said gently again.

Constance tore herself from her chair. "You are not on the same *scale* as my brother!" She came across to me. "You have no *right* to mingle yourself with him, his life, his mistresses, how dare such a— a—*foreigner*"—her face scarlet, possessed, she lurched in front of me, slapping my face—"interfere here! My brother is superior, superior, unique among men! You *dare!* You!" Her hand was caught this time by Titou.

"Stop," he said in a voice full of shame. "We know you're in love with Uncle," in a furious whisper, "we've always known."

She turned and looked at him with a stricken face, with awe, and then beginning to cough or sob she made her way almost painfully, almost as though suddenly struck old, back to her chair. "Get that man out of the house," she said.

"That man," Marc began—"you exceed yourself, Titou—that man was always, you know, a faithful husband. So I am told by one in a position to know. Position, yes, that's the word. She told me that he was but *iridescently* faithful, matchless, as a matter of fact. Very Catholic, every minute. So touching and old-fashioned!"

Liliane rose slowly out of her chair and brought her left fist clutching the napkin down on the table with a force that rattled the china.

"*I'm not that bad!*" she cried, swaying slightly, flushed, "*I'm not that bad!*"

"What are you saying?" Marc said.

"Do you suppose I would have stayed with you," she began rapidly, moving swiftly around the table toward him, "if I thought I *deserved* anything better, if for a second I thought I could *merit* anything better! Don't be ridiculous! No one on earth"—then pausing in her flight for a reflective moment—"no one except it seems your sister—no one would stay with *you!* You've been *dead* for fifteen years, do you understand? and nothing survives except the wish to kill in you, so who would stay with you? Oh, my God, I'm *not* that bad! I'm not, I know I'm not, I know it, I feel it, there *are* things in me—I know there are, I feel them! Oh, thank God, I'm *not* that bad, oh, thank God!"

"You simply forgive yourself for the parade of lovers during your marriage. That was nothing."

"I was afraid," she said quickly, shaking her black hair slightly, "terribly afraid. I couldn't help it; well, I could help it, perhaps I could help it, but I could not help being *terribly afraid.* I thought, you know," taking a deep breath, looking away from him, out through the low, wide, open window over the garden and into the lights and night of the Mediterranean, "I thought that love, a physical presence next to me, I thought that would make me feel safe. Only one other thing ever did, music. That's all, and aside from that I had this presence of fear always with me and love *did* make me feel safe; it worked, it lasted for a while, it helped. And then, yes," turning back to him, "then I would find another man and another, yes, and why not?" Her chin came up a little, "Why not?" Then her expression altered and she turned slowly toward me, "Except that you, my darling, you didn't like it." She slowly began to advance to me. "You didn't like it, and that was because you loved me. So that way of finding safety became a nightmare, because you see I loved you, yes, I loved you."

"And yet," I said in a low voice, "you didn't feel safe with me."

"No," she said gently, "no."

How could she have? I asked myself slowly. I had no courage for her. How could she have?

"What a night!" she said. "I must get out of here, leave." Rummaging among her feelings, she was talking quickly, "Oh, thank God, it's as though I'd been buried in sand."

I took her hand. "You're coming with me."

"You," she said, out of breath, "you don't want me. You don't want to risk me again," looking closely at me.

Jeannot's courage had been to do what he felt deeply in his heart.

"Yes," I said, "yes, I do, yes."

Her face, fragile and tanned, with a certain liquid quality about her eyes and hair, her face turned radiant then and she said suddenly: "Do you know, this has been a perfect dinner! Perfect. I can't tell you. How do you manage to achieve this atmosphere? So goodbye, Monsieur Marc; thank you again, Constance, Titou, *au revoir*, and remember, De Gaulle to power! Let me stress, never has there been such a dinner! Never!" I started with her out of the dining room.

"I hope you'll be happy," said Titou suddenly, and almost tremulously, gazing with a piteous look at us.

"They won't be together a week," said Marc. "She'll be on the streets," he added, turning disgustedly away, "and he'll be in a nervous crisis."

Liliane whirled. "I don't believe it," she said. "What I always really feared most was a relationship as detestable as the one I've had with you. So now I've experienced the worst."

Out we went, through the living room and out into the Mediterranean night. "I don't believe it," Liliane repeated, half to herself.

||||||||||||||||||||

I had come for her. I had not gone away, I had come for her. Not an act of golden courage, not like giving up your life for what lies deeply in your heart; but just a short but definite and irrevocable step. Since I had never walked that way in my life, the first step could only be a short one.

A few days later the French people in an atmosphere of great order and calmness overwhelmingly approved the Fifth Republic of General de Gaulle. The disorders all over France immediately ceased. That was the day Liliane and I left Antibes for Paris. Driving north along the National Route, I thought of Jeannot, making his way south to find a national route of his own.

Now that he was no longer here I could see and understand him more clearly. I realized that under his dark North African skin, behind his Arab eyes, deeper than his violent Mediterranean gestures, truer than his Moslem elusiveness, there was a young man, a being. When you said North African and Arab and Mediterranean and Moslem you had not defined him; you had only traced his outline. The center, the essence lay deeper than all these categories; he was too much himself, too specifically Jeannot to be defined by them; at the same time his nature struggled instinctively to go beyond them, to fuse with larger unities, to merge with all other categories— Nordic and Japanese and Presbyterian, for instance. And the crude battering prow of this drive, with him and all of us, was engulfing desire, was love.

It worked very badly. Love doesn't conquer, not always, not usually, hardly ever. But it fights.

RENEWALS 458-4574

DATE DUE

NOV 15			

GAYLORD

PRINTED IN U.S.A.